AMPLE PORTIONS

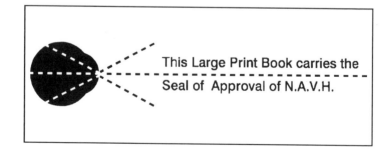

This Large Print Book carries the
Seal of Approval of N.A.V.H.

OHIO BOOK 3

AMPLE PORTIONS

THE YOUNG BUCKEYE STATE BLOSSOMS WITH LOVE AND ADVENTURE IN THIS COMPLETE NOVEL

DIANNE CHRISTNER

THORNDIKE PRESS

An imprint of Thomson Gale, a part of The Thomson Corporation

THOMSON

GALE

Detroit • New York • San Francisco • New Haven, Conn. • Waterville, Maine • London

LIBRARY OF CONGRESS CATALOGING-IN-PUBLICATION DATA

Christner, Dianne L., 1951–
    Ample portions : the young Buckeye State blossoms with love and adventure in this complete novel / by Dianne Christner.
        p. cm. — (Ohio ; bk. 3) (Thorndike Press large print Christian historical fiction)
    ISBN-13: 978-0-7862-9782-5 (alk. paper)
    ISBN-10: 0-7862-9782-4 (alk. paper)
    1. Ohio — Fiction. 2. Sisters — Fiction. 3. United States — History — 1783–1865 — Fiction. 4. Large type books. I. Title.
    PS3603.H76A83 2007
    813'.6—dc22   2007018177

Published in 2007 by arrangement with Barbour Publishing, Inc.

Printed in the United States of America on permanent paper
10 9 8 7 6 5 4 3 2 1

With love to my children,
Mike and Rachel.
May God richly bless your lives
with His ample portions.

CHAPTER 1

A single provocative curl — long, brunette, and tousled — dangled from Miriam Wheeler's otherwise ribbon-tied tresses and captivated her husband. As she spoke, the curl partially concealed her worry-wrinkled brow, but Luke easily detected frustration in the tone of her voice.

"The man's behavior was insufferable! He was probably drunk. . . ." Miriam paused to tug at the ends of her apron strings, which would not stretch nowadays to meet across her veritably pregnant middle. Luke's mirthful eyes and the crooked grin spreading across his face did not deter her. Letting the ties drop and setting swollen hands upon the proximity of her hips, she sighed. "Be serious, Luke."

Smiling mischievously, he reached a ready hand to tuck the distracting ringlet back into place and maintained. "I'm trying, Miriam."

Resisting his playful mood, she continued. "Think of his poor wife. For Aaron to insult you, a parson, in such a manner must be humiliating for Ruth. Luke, won't you call on the Gateses tomorrow and resolve this misunderstanding? For her sake?"

The preacher succumbed easily to his wife's beseeching brown eyes which, as always, melted his reserve until no request was too big. He pulled her close. "Of course, Darling," he whispered, "if it means so much to you."

It was the last promise Luke Wheeler made to his wife Miriam before her death. For several weeks he completely forgot about it — but today he had suddenly remembered.

As the young widower stuffed clothes into a black valise, he spoke softly to his two-month-old son, Davy. "I made a promise to your mama, and I need to keep it." Exhaling a weary sigh, he continued. "Just this one last thing, then tomorrow we head for Beaver Creek. It's time you met your relatives."

Davy's newborn arms flailed through the air, and he wailed, his face beet red. Luke picked up the infant that mirrored his own characteristics, stroking the cornsilk hair. "Please don't object. Don't you see? My heart's not in the ministry since . . ." His voice faded.

He remembered accepting his first pastorate job with such enthusiasm two years earlier. That was the year the missionary's daughter swept him off his feet. Accompanying her father on a visit to the States, Miriam had been equally captivated by the new Presbyterian preacher — so much so that before her father returned to the mission field the following spring, she and Luke were married.

The two years that followed were no less than glorious. Luke gave his all to the ministry, supported lovingly by his young wife. Their days were filled with hard work, lightened with laughter, and seasoned with love. But now . . .

Grief marked Luke's worn face with an inconsolable expression. Large grooves cut downward through his cheeks, hidden in part by a yellow mustache. The days when dimples danced there, dodging laughter and smiles, were gone. Today dark circles framed his blue eyes, making him look older than his twenty-five years.

"My brain's fuzzy as a cobweb." He continued. "I feel empty, so far away from God." The baby settled down at the subdued tones of his father's voice, sticking a fist into his mouth to suck. Luke caressed the small face with his thumb, outlining Davy's velvety cheek, pink and perfect. "Hungry again?"

That same afternoon the rhythmic canter of Queenie, Luke's quarter horse, soothed father and child alike. Those living in Dayton, Ohio, in the summer of 1810, took this unusual sight for granted — the giant good-looking widower toting his pint-sized son. Teary-eyed females often paused to sigh at the poignant reminder of Luke's loss.

When they reached the lodgings of Claire Larson, Luke dismounted, confident that he could go to her today with his need. As he walked toward the house with Davy, he thought back over the years that he had known her.

Claire, whose parents had been killed in the Big Bottom Indian massacre of 1791, grew up in Beaver Creek, Ohio, under the care of her Aunt Mattie. When Claire was twelve, Luke's brother Ben married Mattie's daughter, making Claire and Luke cousins.

Claire became a Christian about the time Luke left Beaver Creek to attend seminary in Dayton. They corresponded, and Luke became Claire's spiritual mentor. During this time, the young woman bombarded

Luke with many questions about her new-found faith.

After seminary, Luke went to work at Dayton's orphanage. On Claire's sixteenth Christmas, she and her family visited Luke there. An orphan herself, Claire was touched in a profound way by the children. Thus she set out to convince her family of her desire to work at the orphanage. For three years she served there, even after Luke went into the pastorate and married Miriam.

As Luke knocked on Claire's door, he reflected that his cousin was no ordinary girl. Her exuberance and warmhearted nature, constant as the sun's warmth on a summer day, provided the stability he so needed during these days when his world seemed to be crumbling down around him.

The moment Claire opened the door, she swept Davy away from Luke, crooning over the child. In response, Luke's blond mustache twitched just as it always did before it curled upward with a smile.

Claire first examined Davy at arm's length before bringing him to her breast for a long cuddle. "Oh, what a little doll you are! And you're getting so big." Only then did she turn her attention to the grinning parent. "Forgive my manners, Luke. Do come in." He followed her swishing skirts into the parlor, where she asked, "What brings you around?"

Luke eased into a stiff chair, tight and squatty beneath his tall, slim form, which had become even thinner since Miriam's death. He leaned forward to prop his elbows on knees elevated high off the ground. "I wasn't sure if I'd catch you at home, but I was coming this way and wondered if you could take care of Davy for a few hours."

"I'd love to!" Her blue eyes reflected genuine delight that Luke had remembered it was her day off from her orphanage job.

Relieved, Luke returned to his feet. "Great!" He lost no time unbuckling a small leather pouch he wore strapped across his chest. "Here's his bottle and some diapers." He held it out before him.

Claire's infant-filled arms remained clasped in their cradled position as she responded with a tilt of her head and a soft chuckle. "Put it there, Luke, on the table."

He missed the humor in his actions, his thoughts focusing mainly on his nagging mission. "I'm on my way to call on the Gateses — not a visit I'm relishing. Tell you all about it later.

"Oh, there's something else, too." Claire's eyes widened expectantly. Fidgety, Luke recovered his hat from the arm of his chair and mechanically dusted it. "Looks like I'll be leaving Dayton sooner than I thought." A quick glance her way revealed Claire's brows arched in consternation, just as he had expected. "We'll talk later. I'll be back before dark."

With hasty strides Luke made for the doorway. He had dreaded telling her of his plans. She had taken it hard when he first shared his decision to leave the ministry, even trying to dissuade him.

Not to be left hanging like that, however, Claire quickly followed, babe in arms, and touched a hand to his sleeve. In a tone revealing deep emotion and concern for his well-being, she said, "I'll look forward to that talk, Luke. God go with you." His departure left her staring after him with many unanswered questions.

As Luke traveled toward his destination, he thought about his promise to Miriam regarding the man called Aaron Gates. An involuntary shudder of disgust swept over him when he recalled his last encounter with the man the day it all began, at the general store. Luke had unexpectedly bumped into Ruth Gates and recognized her as a woman who attended his church sporadically, always slipping into the back pew after the service started and leaving before it was over. Naturally, he was excited to make her acquaintance and greeted her with the irrepressible enthusiasm of a young pastor. No wonder then, his mouth fell agape when Ruth's husband appeared a few steps behind her with a malicious sneer planted on his tanned jowls. Muttering vile accusations, he seemed determined to pick a fight.

Luke's disbelief had turned to anger when the man thrust his wife aside, causing her to stumble backwards. Beneath the plaid shirt untucked from the man's exertion, bulging arms rippled from muscles toned at sea. Although Luke's nerves bristled and small beads of sweat broke out upon his brow, he did not cower under Aaron Gates's stormy stare. The reddened, glazed-over eyes told the tale. He was drunk.

His loud, slurry voice had caused a scene before the store's other customers. "Keep your sweet talk to yourself, Preacher, and leave my wife alone!" The accusation embarrassed Luke, and he had stammered a futile apology while the intoxicated man pushed past him, knocking several items off the shelf as he stomped out of the shop.

"I'm so sorry, Reverend," Ruth Gates mumbled before she also fled.

When Luke had told Miriam about the

man's accusations, she had asked him to call upon the Gateses and rectify the situation. However, circumstances had prevented him from fulfilling this promise as the next day his wife took to her bed, and shortly afterward she died in childbirth.

Beset with an excruciating grief which vanquished all else, Luke forgot about the promise. It was a miracle, all things considered, that he could even perform the most mundane duties required of him over the next two months.

But for Davy's sake, Luke had persevered. His son's initial fight for survival was of paramount importance to him, and toward this effort he poured all his remaining energies. Remarkably, Davy flourished under Luke's tender care. During this time, the idea seeded and grew in Luke's heart that he should move back home to Beaver Creek, Ohio. Subsequently he turned in his resignation at the Presbyterian Church where he pastored.

The day finally arrived when he began to pack. In his haste, he snatched his coat from a peg beside the stove when something floated to the floor, catching his eye. *Miriam's apron!* A sudden pang of anguish surfaced when he knelt to pick it up. He tenderly fingered the cloth, remembering how she had outgrown it in those last days.

This cherished memory stirred yet another, troubling Luke and calling up his last promise to Miriam. And though he tried to cast it off, he could not. Finally, he yielded to his conscience, determined to deal with the matter, which eventually brought him to this place — a mile down the road from the Gates farm.

CHAPTER 2

With the June sun scorching his bare neck, Luke approached the shaded dwelling that poked shyly through a curtain of beech trees, and it crossed his mind that in his grief April and May had come and gone without his knowledge. A calico dress billowing on the wash line caught his attention, bringing thoughts of Miriam. Townspeople insisted his late wife resembled Ruth Gates. He considered it now for a fleeting moment, then cast the thought aside. No, the Gates woman was much older, mid-thirties at least.

Drawing nearer, within yards of the Gateses' cabin, Luke was startled by angry shouts; instinctively, he pulled his mount to a halt. Listening closely, he picked up fragments of what sounded like men arguing. *What a time I picked to call!* he thought. *But I have to fulfill my promise to Miriam.*

Thus Luke steeled himself to face his

obligation as he dismounted and tethered his horse to the closest sapling. Proceeding with caution, he headed toward the house, fully expecting to receive the brunt end of Aaron Gates's bulging biceps.

When he was a few steps onto the porch, however, the shouting ceased, creating a sudden eerie quiet that magnified the creaking of the boards beneath his boots. Luke raised his fist to knock, but upon hearing the pitiful cry of a woman, he instinctively thrust open the door with both hands and let it slam against the wall. It took his eyes a moment to adjust to the dim interior. When they did, his mind rebelled against the horror of the scene even as his body played into action.

Within five feet to the left of a long plank table, Aaron Gates lay in a bloody pool on the cabin floor. Without a second thought, Luke crossed the short distance to kneel beside the ashen-faced man. Ruth Gates, who was already bent over her husband, reached up to clutch Luke's sleeve as she begged, "Please, help us!"

Though Aaron appeared lifeless, Luke immediately snatched his hanky from his back pocket and positioned it over the wound on the back of the man's head. "Can you hold this in place?" he asked Ruth. At her nod, he worked quickly to bring the loose ends around Aaron Gates's head, pulling it tight to stop the profuse bleeding.

Rousing slightly now, Aaron began to thrash about, but Luke restrained the injured man by cradling his head against his own chest. The preacher's mind raced wildly, his temples pounding. Nevertheless, outwardly he appeared calm and rational. *Keep him still and stop the bleeding,* he thought. *Must get a doctor. Ruth can't . . . What? Hoofbeats?* Luke cocked his head to listen. But before he could investigate the source of that sound, Aaron Gates required his attention once again. He gasped, struggling — then finally collapsed, limp within Luke's strong grip.

With that Ruth shrieked, "Do something!"

Frantically probing the man's neck, Luke searched for a pulse, knowing even as he did so, it was too late. Seeing the look on her benefactor's face, Ruth grew strangely quiet, her eyes darting from him to her husband and back, her breath held.

Luke, too, was silent as he gently laid the man onto the wooden floor before he turned his attention back to Ruth. "I'm sorry, Ma'am, he's gone," he said, flinching at her scream.

"No! No! He can't be."

Luke reached out to comfort her, but she recoiled in fear. Puzzled, for the first time he really looked at her. It was then he noticed the woman's swollen face, blackening near the cheekbone. With increasing realization, he identified, too, the smell of alcohol permeating the corpse. In that same instant, he knew she had been the victim of abuse.

Thinking that he understood better now, the young preacher spoke in soothing tones, using her given name. "Ruth, I'm sorry. I'll help you with this. It's going to be all right."

Ruth lifted her eyes and held Luke's compassionate gaze before she swiped at her tears with her apron and moved into his arms. He consoled her as she wept, whispering a prayer for the situation.

Eventually she calmed a bit, and Luke gently placed her at arm's length, gripping her shoulders in support. "I want to help, Ruth," he said, his eyes warm and caring. "Can you tell me what happened here?" Upon hearing that question, the look in the woman's eyes grew wild.

"Ruth, you can trust me," Luke urged. But before she could answer, a shadow fell across the floor from behind them, and Luke jerked his head around to see who had entered the room. The Gateses' neighbor,

Uriah Cook, stood in the open doorway, taking in the scene. Instantly Ruth tore free from Luke's restraint and flung herself upon the newcomer, screaming, "Help me! Oh, help me! The preacher's killed Aaron!"

Luke gasped his surprise, "What? Why the woman must be in shock!" Then a gut-wrenching foreboding gripped him as he watched Ruth's convincing performance.

She thrust a finger at Luke, spewing out accusations. "It was awful, Uriah! He came here, said he was looking for his wife, Miriam . . . that he was so glad he found me, and then he . . . Oh, it was terrible." Ruth sobbed into her hands, leaving Uriah to eye Luke warily, noting the other's bloodied shirt and hands. "Go on," he urged. "I won't let him harm you."

"He came after me, but I fought him off, and then he hit me." She gingerly placed her hand to the swollen spot on her cheek.

"That is ridiculous!" Luke exploded, finally having the sense to intervene on his own behalf.

Uriah's face grew flinty, and he pulled his gun from his holster pointing it at the towering preacher. "Shut up and stay put, or I'll put a bullet in your head! You'll get your say." He turned back to his neighbor. "Go on, Mrs. Gates."

She paused a moment, then replied, "He hit me, and then Aaron came in. They struggled, and the next thing I knew my poor husband lay on the floor bleeding. The preacher grabbed me again; then there you were, standing in the doorway."

Ruth turned toward Luke and hissed, "Though you're a man of the cloth, I despise ya!" She spat at the floor and lunged forward while Uriah reached out to restrain her from railing at Luke.

"Let me handle this, Ruth," Uriah said, taking charge. "You sit down now and try to calm yourself." After the woman obediently sank onto a chair, Uriah Cook waved his pistol at Luke and bent slowly over the body to verify that his friend was indeed dead. With this confirmed, he looked at Luke. "All right, easy now, Preacher. I'll be taking you into town to see the sheriff. Now, move!"

"But that's my hanky around his head. I only tried to help. You've got to believe me; I had nothing to do with this," Luke argued.

"Look, I don't know how that got there. All I know is there'll be plenty of time to sort it out 'cause you're gonna be telling your story to Sheriff Watson." Then Uriah turned toward Mrs. Gates and added, "You'd better come along, too."

Ruth's face turned chalky. "I–I can't. Why, my children will be home shortly. They're at the neighbor's seeing a new litter of puppies. I can't let them find their pa this way!"

Uriah had to agree, "You're right. They shouldn't have to see such a spectacle. I'll stop at my place on the way and send the wife over to help you."

Ruth's color returned with her sigh of relief. "Thank you. You're a good neighbor, Uriah."

Having no choice, Luke did not resist Uriah when the man poked his gun into his ribs, motioning him outside. Still incredulous, however, the preacher glanced over his shoulder at the woman who had lied so persuasively, but in return, she met his eyes with a hard look, and all he could do was hang his head. *Lord, what is going on? Why is my whole world crumbling around me. Have You forsaken me?*

Luke stepped into the empty cell and flinched when the steel door slammed shut behind him. He wheeled about just in time to see the red-haired lawman twist the key into the padlock and drop it into a deep vest pocket before he cast Luke a final look and turned away.

Like liquid fear, panic coursed through

Luke's bloodstream. *Trapped!* He gripped the iron bars and pulled, but the barricade remained immovable. He jerked until his hands felt bruised and the dangling lock rattled.

Surprised at his prisoner's unruly behavior, Sheriff Watson reappeared. "Hey now, Rev. Wheeler, that won't do. You'll wear yourself out. Better just rest up for tomorrow," he cautioned.

Luke's hands slipped downward until they relaxed and fell limp at his sides. He felt the lawman's watchful gaze as a thought struck him. *The sheriff probably thinks I am insane, just like Ruth Gates described me. I must control myself.* Thoroughly dejected, Luke nodded to the lawman, then let his eyes peruse the ten-by-ten-foot cell interior.

To his left, a small bare cot — too short for Luke's tall body — lined the wall. Straight ahead, Luke saw a barred window at chest level. With disdain, he eyed the pewter pot placed against the adjoining dirty wall.

After the quick inspection, he crossed the tiny cell and bent to look out. Facing east, he discerned the sketchy outline of a river embankment, a small portion of the Miami River. The view was a hazy gray, however, as the sun already hung low, and beyond, a fog hovered.

Nevertheless, Luke's heart gladdened with this tiny measure of freedom. *At least I can watch the river traffic!* With the thought came a gentle assurance, and he expelled a sigh. *The very river where I baptize converts. Thank You, Lord.* He crooked his neck and stared out the iron-barred square-foot opening until the stars appeared. Then, breathing in the fresh air as if it were a rationed commodity, Luke poured out his heart to God.

The next morning Luke collected his thoughts. *Need to get a lawyer, find someone to take care of Davy until I can get out of here. . . .* His mental list dispelled as obscure voices drifted into his cell from the outer room. He moved to the bars, straining to hear. Thus, the pitiful scene which greeted his visitor when the outer door swung open was Luke's unshaven face pressed against the bars with his hands gripping the cold iron like a criminal.

Claire gasped, and her hands flew to cover her mouth as she stifled a sob.

"Claire!" Luke exclaimed, overwhelmed with emotion.

Sheriff Watson briefly touched the small woman's elbow. "Are you all right, Miss?"

It took Claire a moment to recover. "Yes.

I–I'm fine."

"You sure?"

Claire nodded. "May I have some time alone with Rev. Wheeler?"

"Wait here, Ma'am." The lawman left the area and returned momentarily with a chair that he placed just outside Luke's cell. "Call me when you're ready to leave," he said before leaving them unattended.

Claire seated herself carefully while she examined Luke's condition. His tear-smudged face was puffy around the eyes, and his shirt, wrinkled and dirty, hung outside his trousers. While Claire searched in vain for the right words, an awkward silence prevailed.

"I'm sorry, Claire. This is no place for a lady." He indicated the cell, feebly waving his hand.

With this gesture, Claire noticed that what she had thought to be soil on his shirt was actually bloodstains. Tears trickled down her cheeks as she reached for him. "Oh, Luke," she cried. "Is it true they've charged you with murder?"

He grasped both her hands through the bars and held onto them as tightly as one clinging to a life preserver in the midst of a stormy sea. "I've been wrongly accused, Claire."

"I worried all night after the deputy brought me word."

"I haven't slept much either," Luke admitted. "I'm glad you came."

She nodded, her smile tremulous. "Tell me what happened, Luke."

"All right." He released Claire's hands to position himself cross-legged before her on the floor. Expelling a great sigh, he began his story.

Claire listened intently as Luke recounted the details leading up to his arrest. Then she tilted her head, looking thoroughly perplexed. "I don't understand. If this occurred as you say, of which I have no doubt, then why are you here?"

Luke shrugged, holding his hands up in helplessness. "The woman lied. And what an actress she was! Framed me good."

Claire shook her bonneted head. Shafts of sunlight from the barred window warmed her face. "How could anyone believe you would do such a thing?" she asked in disbelief.

Luke sobered. "Claire, I don't know, but they do. Will you help me?"

"Of course. What can I do?" She leaned close to the bars, eager to assist in any way.

"Simon Appleby — I want him to be my lawyer. Can you ask him to drop by?"

27

"Yes. I'll go right away." She started to rise but was stayed by a gentle hand reaching through the bars.

"Wait, Claire. How's Davy?"

A sweetness lit the young woman's face. "He's just fine, Luke. Don't you worry. I'll take good care of your baby boy."

"I know it's a lot to ask of you, but he's all I have left. He means so much to me and —"

Claire covered his hand where it rested on the bars. "Hush now, Luke. Caring for Davy is no bother. You know I love him."

Luke's countenance softened for a moment, then turned troubled again. "If I don't get out of this, will you take Davy to my brother, Ben?"

Claire stiffened. "Of course, but don't even say such a thing, Luke. You'll soon be free. I'll get Mr. Appleby over here first thing. He'll know what to do."

Luke said, "You know, I was angry with God when Miriam died. I truly didn't believe things could get any worse. But now I find myself on my knees again. I can't say I have a peace about this, but I know He's here with me."

"Then God will keep you strong. Believe it!"

His smile was weak. "Claire, thank you

for coming."

The young woman dabbed at her eyes with her lace handkerchief as Luke called out, "Sheriff Watson!"

The lawman's bulky physique appeared so quickly that Luke realized he had been waiting just beyond the door. Afterward Luke sank thoughtfully onto his cot. Having shared with Claire, a true sister in faith, his burden felt lighter. He was finally able to close his eyes to rest.

Chapter 3

Claire twisted long golden strands of hair into a pleasing arrangement, tightly bound at the nape of her slender neck. As she took careful inventory of herself, the looking glass reflected serious blue eyes set in a pale oval face with strong cheekbones sloping downward toward a button chin. Today she did not pinch her cheeks to force a flow of color, but rather with her fingertips traced the collar of the black dress. It fit her mood — dark and bleak. The dress gave her an air of sophistication that surpassed her nineteen years. This day she needed to be treated with serious regard. Luke was depending on her.

Turning from her reflection, she lifted Davy from her bed and smiled down at his beaming face. His cuddly presence warmed her as she started down the stairs and toward the dining room where the aroma of bacon and eggs wafted through the air.

Claire's landlady was bent over a plate of hot biscuits, but upon hearing Claire, she raised her head, revealing round cheeks flushed from the stove's heat. "Morning, Child. How did Davy sleep last night?"

"Better. But I think he misses his papa." Claire gave the baby an affectionate squeeze.

"Yes, I'm sure he does." Mary Anders's expression brightened upon seeing her bald-headed Swedish husband, Gustaf, standing at the door dressed in his town clothes.

"Sorry if I'm holding you up," he said to Claire. "I went ahead and got the rig ready to go."

"Not at all," Claire answered politely. She and the older couple, members of the same Presbyterian congregation where Luke served as pastor, shared a common concern.

Gustaf pulled up a chair, while with his free hand he reached out to tickle Davy. "Morning, little one."

At the same time, Mary dished a question out to Claire along with the morning fare. "Sure you don't want me to take care of Davy today while you and Gustaf are busy with errands?"

"That's sweet of you, Mary, but no thanks. I especially want to take him along. I expect it will cheer Luke."

Mary sobered at the mention of Luke's

separation from his child, who had been his primary joy in life since Miriam's death.

"Have you heard when the judge will return to Dayton?" Mary asked.

Gustaf's head jerked up in response to his wife's question, and he focused intently on Claire's reply.

"No. They haven't set a date for the trial yet. Everything is so uncertain. I plan to ask Simon Appleby this morning."

Gustaf nodded. "I'll be meeting this morning with some of the townsmen to discuss ways to help out the reverend. The town's all in an uproar since there's never been a murder trial before. And to think our reverend is a suspect in such a thing!" He shook his head with disbelief.

"Oh, my." Mary's ample bosom heaved as she pulled a handkerchief from her apron pocket to dab at her eyes. "Such a sad thing. What a shame." Turning aside, she sniffled. "Gustaf, be sure to ask Micah Brewer about his wife's list." At her husband's puzzled expression, she added, "The schedule, so folks can take turns cooking the reverend a hot meal. My, my." Once more she shook her head. "I don't know what this world is coming to with folks believing that gentle man could have committed a murder."

The room, which usually brimmed with

life, now fell silent except for the scraping of utensils. Ruffled curtains, oval braided rug, and calico tablecloth — all products of Mary Anders's handiwork — depicted a cheery setting. But today everyone's hearts were heavy with preoccupied thoughts. The squeaking of Gustaf's chair broke the stillness as he rose from the table.

"I'll be waiting outside, Miss Claire."

"Thank you. Davy and I'll just be a moment."

Claire started across the busy street in the direction of the building marked in bold black letters, BARRISTER SIMON APPLEBY. To her relief, the door opened easily when she gave it a push with her shoulder. A middle-aged, dark-haired gentleman rose instantly from his chair.

"Miss Larson!" he greeted. "Please, come in. Sit down. It's a pleasure to see you again."

Once she was settled, Simon Appleby assessed the woman seated across the desk, cradling the tiny son of his friend and client. His manner put Claire at ease.

"Thank you, Mr. Appleby," she said.

"Rev. Wheeler expressed his great appreciation of you." He watched her eyes widen in surprise. "That is, in taking care of

Davy. In fact, he appointed me to look after you both, especially where the child is concerned."

"It's so like him to care about others when he has problems of his own," Claire answered.

"From my experience, folks in jail have plenty of time to think, sort things through."

The crass remark caused Claire to tense, and the baby stirred uncomfortably. "Mr. Appleby, will you be able to help Luke?" she asked, shifting Davy to a better position.

"If it's any consolation, Luke is my friend, too. We go back a ways. I've always admired the young man for his ability in the pulpit, as well as his efforts to provide better conditions at the orphanage. Just as I admire you for your work there, Miss Larson."

He could see Claire relax as he continued. "I intend to devote all my attention to Luke's case in order to prove his innocence." Claire listened as she unconsciously rocked Davy, a gesture not unnoticed by the attentive lawyer. This prompted him to ask, "How have the arrangements been working out with Davy? Are they agreeable?"

"Oh yes! My work at the orphanage remains unhampered, and I'm growing quite attached to Davy. In fact, I plan to set Luke's mind at ease with a visit just as soon as we're finished here."

Simon's gray-streaked eyebrows arched with concern. "You realize, of course, your caring for the child is only temporary?" he asked.

"Yes. Luke told me he wishes for his brother, Ben, to be Davy's true guardian. But surely it won't come to that? Do you have any idea when the trial will be?" Claire drew his thoughts back to the matter at hand.

Simon shook his head. "No. The date's not set as yet. That's to our advantage, however. It'll give me time to build my case."

"I want to thank you so much for all you are doing for Luke. If anything happens to him, I . . ."

Simon leaned across the desk, professionally covering Claire's hand with his own. "I understand, Miss Larson."

"I don't know, Ma'am." Sheriff Watson's stern voice along with his disapproving scowl sent Claire's heart racing. "This isn't a place for a child."

"Please, Sheriff, just give Luke a few minutes to see his son."

"With the way folks are flitting in and out, you'd think this was a social event," he growled, referring to Luke's parishioners. "It just ain't proper."

Claire's lip trembled as she breathed a prayer and simply asked again, "Please?"

"Oh, all right. But if he cries, you'll have to go." He quickly turned his back to the young woman lest she see the emotion in his eyes. "Come on." He tossed over his shoulder.

Claire followed, now accustomed to the procedure of the outer door swinging open to reveal a vulnerable and unsuspecting prisoner. Today her first glimpse of the preacher bent over his open Bible filled her with relief. Luke jumped to his feet upon seeing her. "Davy!"

Sheriff Watson shook his bushy carrot-topped head but retreated to his usual post just outside the door without further comment.

To Luke's delight, Davy responded with enthusiasm to his father's familiar voice and face. "He hasn't forgotten his pa." Luke's words broke, filled with emotion.

"Of course not!" Claire bounced the excited baby, while holding him close to Luke. She placed a tiny fist between the bars.

Luke rolled Davy's fragile fingers with the tips of his own. The gesture caused Claire's heart to ache. She waited patiently, allowing Luke to savor these moments with his son.

After a few minutes, she spoke softly. "He's adjusted nicely, sleeping through the night now."

"Did you get his cradle from the house?"

"Yes. It's right beside my bed." Claire's cheeks flamed as Luke considered this.

He gently reprimanded her. "Sounds like you're spoiling him."

"Not any more than you," she contended.

Luke shrugged. "I guess I have lavished him with love, all that I had to give." His expression turned melancholy.

The tiny cell area grew quiet until Claire spoke reassuringly. "Luke, I just know that the truth will come out, and you'll be acquitted. Mr. Appleby assured me he is devoting all his time to your case. And God is faithful. He will hear our prayers."

But Luke's dismal mood remained fixed. "I've been so lonely since Miriam died, I'd just as soon join her." His tone, so dejected, frightened Claire.

"No, Luke. Please don't say that."

He avoided her pleading eyes as he voiced his haunting fear. "You realize I might hang."

"Dayton's never had a hanging. Anyway, they wouldn't hang an innocent man!" At Claire's raised pitch, Davy reached out to grab at her cheek, and she unconsciously removed his hand with a gentle gesture while intently searching Luke's face.

He met her gaze unwaveringly, his pain obvious. "Listen, Claire. I haven't lost my faith in God, but you just don't understand what it's like to feel so empty, so alone —"

Claire interrupted. "Perhaps not, but you cannot give up. You will get out of here, Luke Wheeler!"

"Ahem." The sheriff cleared his throat loud enough to warn them of his approach. "Got your lunch here, Preacher. Looks like another fancy spread, too." Sheriff Watson turned to Claire. "I'm sorry, Ma'am, your time is up."

"Please, I'm not quite ready."

The lawman frowned, considering while he balanced Luke's plate precariously on one age-roughened hand. "One more minute," he growled, then disappeared again.

"I can't leave you this way," Claire protested. She fought back tears of anguish and clung fiercely to Davy, whose small downy head snuggled against her neck.

Knowing that their time together was

short now, Luke obliged Claire. "Hey, now." He reached through the bars to lightly tap her chin. "Who's to say? Perhaps you're right. It's in God's hands after all."

Claire sniffed. "That's better. I know God will make a way." Then she shifted the baby so Luke could get a last look at his son's face.

"Thank you, Claire, for bringing Davy." He struggled with a lump in his throat as the infant's hand trustingly wrapped about his extended finger. "Bye, Davy. I love you, Son."

Claire made a brave attempt at a smile. "God be with you, Luke. Don't give up."

CHAPTER 4

God be with you. Don't give up. Claire's parting words echoed in Luke's head, tormenting him for the remainder of the day. Just when he thought he had settled the matter in his heart, accepted the possibility of the gallows, she flung those scraps of hope at his feet. He had gone so far as to welcome thoughts of joining his beloved Miriam in heaven until Claire brought Davy by and left him with those strong words of encouragement.

Later, much sobered by his thoughts, Luke welcomed Sheriff Watson's announcement. "Got a visitor to see you, Preacher," he said, opening the cell door to admit Luke's lawyer.

"Hello, Simon." Luke rushed forward to shake the man's already extended hand.

"Afternoon, Luke." Simon Appleby waited until the sheriff had procured him a stool and was gone before he spoke again. With the chamber door secured and Sheriff Watson out of sight, he began, "Well, Luke, we have a lot to cover today. Might as well make yourself comfortable."

Luke perched on the edge of his lumpy cot as Simon continued. "I'm going to ask you some pretty hard questions. Got to hear your answers to get the whole picture. The prosecuting attorney will be even rougher than I am today, and you need to be prepared. Understand?"

Luke squared his shoulders, nodding grimly.

"Good. Now, what exactly were your feelings toward Ruth Gates?"

At first the question offended Luke, but then sensing Simon's line of reasoning, he settled himself for the staged interrogation. "I thought of her as a sister in my congregation, with concern for her well-being."

"Isn't it true that she markedly resembles your late wife, Miriam?"

"Some think so," Luke muttered.

"You loved your wife?"

"Very much."

"You miss your wife?"

"Of course I do! More than anything." Luke's face flushed as his raw emotions were set on edge.

Simon was ruthless. "Would you say folks

thought Ruth Gates looked enough like your wife to be her sister?"

Luke glared at Simon, knowing where this was leading.

"I'm sorry, Luke. See what I mean? This will all come out in the trial. It's better to get your initial reactions behind us so you can respond in a controlled manner in the courtroom."

Luke sighed his resignation. "I understand. Let's keep going."

"Would you say Ruth Gates looked enough like your wife to be her sister?"

"Some might think so."

"Did you think so?"

"I never gave it much thought. Like I said, she was just a sister in the congregation."

"Good. Very good, Luke."

"It's just the truth."

"I know, but without the emotional baggage. Now let's start again with the scene itself. What time did you arrive at the Gates farm?"

"I left home about one o'clock in the afternoon and took Davy to Claire Larson's to stay. It must have been about three."

Simon could not resist. "What is your relationship with Miss Larson?"

Luke appeared puzzled but replied quickly, "She's a distant relative."

"Um-hmm." Simon scratched his chin. "How distant?"

"My brother, Ben, married her first cousin, Kate."

"She's not a blood relative then?"

"No, why?"

"She seems very attached to you and Davy."

"Claire won't be brought into this thing, will she?"

"No, no. Don't worry." Simon shook his head and changed the subject. "Let's proceed. Now this is very important, Luke. What exactly did you hear when you arrived at the Gateses'? Try to remember carefully."

Luke hesitated. "Men quarreling."

"Male shouts? Who? Aaron?"

"Yes, I heard his voice."

"What else?"

"There was a woman screaming."

"Ruth Gates?"

"I assume it was her."

"Can you place the other male by his speech?"

Luke hesitated again. "No, I can't identify him."

Simon paused thoughtfully. "You know, Luke, it was probably the killer. Any hunches? Sometimes clues are tucked away in the subconscious but leave impressions that lead directly to the murderer."

Luke shook his head.

"Any signs of a third person, anything that doesn't fit, a glimpse or sound of one fleeing?" Luke thought hard, reliving the scene in his mind. "Think about the way the room looked. What was out of order? What was lying around?"

"A chair was tipped. I had the impression the kitchen was messy, but it wasn't mealtime."

"Did the room smell like anything?"

"Liquor."

"Was there a liquor bottle?"

"I don't recall."

"Think about the way Ruth behaved. Do you believe she could have killed her husband? Perhaps ushered a lover out the back door?"

Luke shook his head. "There's no back door, but the curtain in the kitchen window caught my eye. It was blowing freely."

Simon chewed on the tip of his pen. "Back to Ruth, what was her reaction when you entered the room?"

"She clung to me, pleaded for my help."

"How did you respond?"

"I placed my hanky about the bleeding wound on Aaron's head. Wait a minute!"

"What?"

Luke jumped up from his cot and ran his fingers through his hair, dislodging a tousled lock that fell damp across his brow. "That's when I heard hoofbeats!" Luke shook his head and raised his arms in a gesture of disbelief. "It entirely slipped my mind." Simon gave him a look of encouragement. Luke paced the floor as he continued excitedly, "Someone must have been riding away! And they rode hard and fast!"

Simon punched a fist into his open palm. "Just as I suspected! I don't believe Ruth killed her husband, though it's still a possibility we must not rule out. If someone else was involved in the argument and fled the scene, odds are that person is the killer."

"And Ruth is covering for him," Luke added, slumping back onto the sagging cot. "It must be someone she loves, considering the show she put on. What an actress. She framed me good."

"Don't get discouraged, Luke. This has been a big help. Now it's my job to figure out who she's protecting. I think I'll just pay Ruth Gates a visit."

"Not much to go on, is it?"

Simon rose and patted his friend's shoulder. "It's a start, Luke."

As promised, the following afternoon Simon Appleby called on Ruth Gates. Upon meeting her, Simon was disturbed that the thirty-five-year-old widow was such an attractive and seemingly intelligent woman. This would make her story more believable and weaken Luke's defense.

Ruth's children were home. They ranged in ages from eighteen to seven. The oldest daughter had been working the day her father was killed. The younger ones were at a neighbor's house. The eldest son, Ruben, did not live at home anymore.

As Simon expected, Ruth's response was cold as a December gale and uncooperative as well. He determined, nevertheless, to uncover some shred of evidence, unearth some emotion that might provide a lead. The children, timid yet curious, watched his every move. Simon turned to the youngest standing nearby. "You must miss your pa." The child remained silent, though her eyes grew large and frightened. Then Simon turned to the eleven year old. "It's not your fault that your pa hit your mama."

"I couldn't stop him," Tom defended.

Ruth's eyes narrowed. "That's quite enough, Mr. Appleby! It isn't proper for you to question the children like this!"

"Sorry, Ma'am. I just don't want them to feel at fault, nor you either. If you tell me what really happened, I'll do my best to help."

"I don't know what you mean!"

"We both know Luke Wheeler did not kill your husband. Let me help you."

"Get out!"

He tipped his hat. "Very well. I'll be on my way then. Thank you for your time."

Simon did not leave the premises. Instead he circled the cabin, searching the ground beneath the kitchen window and the area between the house and the barn. Seeing him, Ruth rushed outside to angrily issue a threat. "I'd much appreciate it if you'd remove yourself from my property. It isn't proper, me being a widow and all. I'll get the sheriff to keep you away if need be!"

"That won't be necessary. I'm on my way. I've found what I was looking for." He gestured toward the area recently swept clean by brush. "Good day, Ma'am."

Ruth stood as still and emotionless as a statue, but as soon as the snoop was gone, she sent Tom scooting out the back with a message to be delivered.

Young Tom Gates panted from his long run to the docks by the Miami River where his pa's fishing vessel, the *Hilde,* was anchored. Just before the breathless boy reached the old craft, he caught a glimpse of a long shadow and ducked behind a barrel reeking of fish guts — a familiar stench to the boy who felt at home on the riverfront pier. The lawyer! This would never do. Tom waited, concentrating on long, controlled breaths until his breathing returned to normal.

A quick peek revealed that the dreaded man's back was turned toward him, and the boy sighed with relief when he saw the lawyer engaged in conversation with a small group of fishermen. Making the most of this opportunity, Tom made a mad dash for the deck of the *Hilde,* where he slipped out of sight without making a sound.

Upon finishing his discussion with three old-timers, Simon pivoted to stroll along the docks, visually inspecting the harbor while memorizing every detail. Early evening activity intensified now. He at least had the name of Aaron's fishing sloop. Checking the vessels moored along the shoreline, he scanned each one until he saw the one painted blue with a white stripe beneath the large cursive inscription, *Hilde.* With quick steps he hastened toward her.

"Watch out! Better look where you're goin', mister fancy pants!"

Simon wheeled about. Before him stood a roughneck, dressed in baggy blue trousers and dingy shirt with a soiled blue handkerchief tied about his forehead.

"You talking to me?" Simon inquired.

The other guffawed aloud at the question, revealing a scraggly beard that all but buried his mouth — a dark gap where teeth used to be. Swishing the black juice in his mouth before sending it in a powerful stream within inches of Simon's leather boots, he replied, "Yeah. You got a problem with that?"

"Umm no–o," Simon purposely drawled, replying with a calm that he could see surprised the roughneck. "Do you?"

Matted woolly eyebrows slanted over dark eyes. "May be purty, but I see ya got spunk. I like that."

"Yes, and questions, too. Did you know Aaron Gates by any chance?"

"Whot if I did?"

"He was murdered last week, and my client is wasting in the town jail, an innocent man. I happen to believe that Aaron Gates was a drunk and woman beater. Know anything about that?"

"Probably was. Don't know for a fact. No law against wife beatin', is there? He was gettin' to be a mean old lout, though."

"Why do you say that?"

"Common fact, that's all."

"Would you be willing to testify to that?"

"Nothing to tell. But I know somebody who might."

"And who would that be?"

The larger man scratched his hirsute chin. "Just wonderin' if it'd be worth my while . . ."

"I can't offer money. The law considers such testimony unacceptable."

He shrugged. "Then you're barkin' up the wrong tree with me, Mister! I ain't no tell-tale."

"My office is on First Street, if you change your mind. Nice to meet you, Mr. . . ."

"Didn't say whot my name was, did I now?"

"Well, the sign on my office reads Simon Appleby."

"Won't do me no good, can't read."

Simon cringed at the departing man's coarse laughter.

He then turned his attention back toward the *Hilde,* startled, though not disappointed, at his fortunate timing. Tom Gates was just coming out of the boat's cabin, fingering something shiny. Simon ducked behind some crates, watching as the lad looked up and about to see if the coast was clear before he descended from the vessel and dashed off in a dead run.

The lawyer brushed off a section of the pier closest to the *Hilde* and seated himself. It wouldn't hurt to keep an eye on the vessel to see what else might turn up, just stick around for awhile to chat with the fishermen as they brought in their day's catch.

CHAPTER 5

The tiny cot squeaked and groaned beneath Luke's one-hundred-seventy-pound frame as he thrashed wildly in his sleep. Moaning, tossing, turning as the nightmare seized him, he awoke with a start, bolting upright. Heaving his legs over the side of the bed, he winced as his bare feet hit the damp, night-cold floor. In contrast, his body felt feverish, covered in sweat.

Still caught in the throes of the nightmare, Luke inhaled and exhaled deeply. Terror raced through his heart while with trembling hands he rubbed his neck, where just moments before the rope had constricted painfully, snuffing out his life.

"Oh, God." He wept. "Is this my destiny? Father, please! I don't want to die this way. Davy needs me." Scenes from his dream replayed over and over, haunting him — the suffocating crowd, condemning eyes. He recalled a set of deep blue ones, sorrowful and desperate; then they became faceless and conspicuous from the others. But the following darkness blotted them out, and hopelessness replaced the light as the black hood fell over his face and the rope slipped about his neck.

Luke squeezed his eyes shut to dispel the reality of the images evoked until gently, ever so tenderly, familiar words harkened unto his soul. *"I can do all things through Christ which strengtheneth me."* Lifting his gaze heavenward where dawn's first muted rays filtered through the tiny slatted window, he finally relaxed and retrieved his worn black Bible from beneath his cot. During the past weeks, just to clutch its familiar soft leather binding brought comfort to his fainting soul. Today, as soon as the room lightened enough to read, he would read the rest of that passage.

Meanwhile he breathed another prayer. "Lord, if it's not Your will that I get out of this, I leave Davy in Your charge. Please make a way for him, provide him with Your special care." This brought his thoughts around to Claire, and he wondered why she had not been to visit for several days. *Probably busy at the orphanage,* he thought. *With Davy to take care of now, her responsibilities are even greater. But doesn't she realize how*

Simon walked at a brisk clip, taking long strides in spite of his short legs. The heavy fog allowed the small, dark-suited attorney to pass along the riverfront inconspicuously. Upon reaching the *Hilde,* Simon squinted his eyes. Stroking his groomed mustache with his ringed finger, he scrutinized the vessel.

Well-tuned ears discerned scraps of heated discussion emanating from below the *Hilde*'s deck, and he strained to listen.

"I hope you are satisfied, Clancy!"

"Don't be shoutin' on my lady!"

"What?"

"That's right. She's my ship now! Haw, haw." The sickening guffaw grew louder as two men emerged from the tiny cabin. Through the thick mist surrounding the prow, Simon could only surmise the silhouette of a young man to be Ruben, Aaron and Ruth Gates's oldest son. The other man, his outline not so clearly visible, bobbed with hilarity.

The obscure figure moved closer, bellowing a final remark. "I'll be back for whot's mine tomorrow!" Simon's eyes lit with recognition — the vulgar sea dog from the other day!

Simon planted his polished boots and straightened his broad form to its full five-foot, seven-inch zenith, expecting to be noticed at any time. His skin crawled as the repulsive character swung about and climbed off the boat backwards, pausing to cast a menacing glance about the docks.

The lawyer's gaze never wavered as it fastened onto that one's leering stare, which soon narrowed with recognition. "Well, now if it ain't the fancy snoop again!"

Simon lifted his brows but ignored the slur as he pursued his inquiry. "Did I hear you say that this vessel is yours, Sir?"

"Sir, is it now? Well, I like that. I really do." The man's bearded face twisted into a contortion of glee. "That's right, the rig is mine."

Simon then turned his attention to the younger man stationed at the bow of the *Hilde.* "I was under the impression that this vessel belonged to Aaron Gates," he called out.

"I'm his son. The *Hilde* came to me after his passing." He gestured with his hand. "Just sold it to that one."

"I see. You must be Ruben Gates then." At the confirming nod, the lawyer continued, "I'd like to board the *Hilde* and have a look around. Which one of you gentlemen wants to accompany me?"

Ruben Gates scowled. "Why? What's the problem?"

"Pardon me." Simon moved closer toward the edge of the dock where the *Hilde* bobbed. "My name is Simon Appleby, Luke Wheeler's attorney."

Fleetingly an unrecognizable emotion swept over Ruben's face, but the young man recovered quickly. "I've nothing to hide. Come aboard, though I don't know what good it can do." Then with displeasure he called to the other seaman, "It'll be ready tomorrow, Clancy. Don't bring your grimy face around 'til noon."

Clancy grumbled and shuffled away, wanting no part of the interrogation about to take place.

Once aboard, Simon questioned young Gates. "I didn't see you at the funeral, didn't think you were in town."

Ruben shrugged noncommittally. "Just got into Dayton. I couldn't get here in time for Father's funeral."

"I see. I'm sorry about your father."

The boy's face flushed, then turned angry. "Then why are you defending his murderer?"

"That's why I'm here. You see, I don't believe Luke Wheeler killed your father,

Ruben."

Ruben's wind-chapped face reddened further. "How can that be? You forget my mother saw the preacher do it?"

"So she says."

"Why should she lie?" Ruben yelled doubling his hand into a hard fist.

"That's what I'm here to find out. Now, may I have a look around?"

Ruben slowly unclenched his fist and extended his arm to gesture permission. "Go ahead," he growled, his steely eyes boring daggers through Simon.

Unwilling to assist in any way, Ruben perched on a railing, watching the lawyer search the vessel, prodding here — examining there.

A long half hour later, Simon was escorted off the *Hilde* empty-handed.

"I'll see you at the hearing?" Simon inquired, dusting himself off.

"Of course. I plan to stick around to see the preacher hanged."

Simon bit back a retort. "Thanks for the tour." In afterthought he added, "By the way, I don't know what you got for the *Hilde,* but I believe Clancy got a bargain. He sure left with a mighty big smile on his face."

Without a reply, Ruben whirled about and stalked away, disappearing down the small ship's cave-like cubicle.

Simon grinned mischievously, rubbed his smooth-shaven chin, and headed toward Main Street to the jailhouse.

As Simon entered the jail's office, Sheriff Watson looked up from his desk. "Howdy, Simon."

"Rusty, can I see my client?"

"Sorry, but he's got another visitor just now. And she's much prettier than you." Sheriff Watson scowled. "This jail's never seen so many visitors before the preacher came."

Simon arched his round dark brows with interest.

"I suppose you want to wait?"

"No." Simon began to leave, then paused as he cast an inquiring look at the sheriff. "Don't suppose you plan to reveal who this pretty lady is?"

"Claire Larson." The sheriff grunted.

"Just tell Luke I stopped by. I'll be back later on my way home." When the broad of Simon's back was fully toward the lawman, a smile softened his face.

Meanwhile, within the jail Claire's presence dispelled the gloom of incarceration. Her lilting voice and tinkling laughter saturated Luke's cell.

"I wish I could have seen that," Luke

remarked, his eyes crinkled at the corners, warm with the light of shared humor.

"He certainly has captured the hearts of all the children. Why, when you're . . . ," Claire hesitated to find the correct words, ". . . free, you'll have to bring Davy to visit the children again, and see for yourself."

"I'd like that. Seems like a long time since I've been to the orphanage." His voice turned husky. "The last few months seem like years."

Claire nodded. She rose from her seat.

"I must return now, but it's been good to see you in such high spirits, Luke. I'll stop in as often as I can. I've been busy at work. We have a new addition, a ten-year-old boy who has attached himself to me like moss. After a difficult start, I believe he's finally adjusting. . . ."

Claire continued talking, but all of a sudden Luke could not hear her — all he could do was see. *Her eyes. They're the ones in my dream! Lord! What are you trying to tell me?*

"Luke?" Claire whispered. "What is it? You wanted to ask me something?"

Luke blinked. "No, no — I was just thinking about a dream I had. Actually, it was a nightmare. But never mind that. You were saying that you've been busy at the orphanage."

"Yes."

"Claire, thank you for coming. I get so lonely here. Having you is like visiting with family. Speaking of which, I have a letter here for my brother, Ben. And one for Miriam's father. Will you post them for me?"

"Of course. Isn't Miriam's father overseas?"

"Yes, he's serving at the same missionary post." Luke reached under his cot, where he kept the few items the sheriff allowed him within the cell, and pulled out the two letters.

As she reached for them through the bars, he clasped her hand. "Claire . . ."

When he did not finish but only murmured her name, she quickly covered his hand with her free one. For one fleeting instant, she felt the depth of his pain, his hopelessness. "I know," was all she could offer. "I know, Luke."

He nodded, then withdrew his hand and thanked her again for coming.

As she rose to leave, she waved the letters. "I'll post these, and, Luke, you have many people praying for you. Keep trusting."

"I will."

"Good-bye then."

"Bye, Claire. Give Davy a kiss for me."

At the word "kiss," Claire lowered her eyes. "Yes, I will."

Pulled by an exquisite chestnut bay, Simon Appleby held the reins taut, maneuvering his small carriage beneath the cool umbrella of a spreading cottonwood tree. Wet in his gentleman's suit, he took just a moment to savor the shade and slight breeze that evaporated the moisture beads gathered over his brow. But his investigative curiosity soon overpowered his need for comfort. He was anxious to examine his newest lead — Claire Larson's urgent summons regarding some important evidence.

Simon hastened toward the sprawling but dismal stone building where he noted clusters of children playing in the fringes of a sun-parched lawn. Claire happened to answer his knock, and upon laying eyes on Simon, relief washed over her face.

"Mr. Appleby! Come in!"

Her excitement contagious, Simon answered, "I got your message. I came as fast as I could."

"Thank you." Claire led Simon down a hallway and into a large parlor as she said, "I think I've stumbled onto something important that may help Luke."

Simon's eyes remained riveted to his

hostess's face, rosy-cheeked with expectation, as he seated himself upon the badly worn Windsor chair she offered him.

Without hesitation, Claire poured forth her information. "We've taken in a most precious boy whose name is Clay. Anyway, as we played with Davy one day, we got on the subject of the Gates murder, and the boy revealed some astounding information."

Simon's forehead creased all the way to the center part of his neatly combed hair. "Go on," he urged.

"You see, the boy was a stowaway from Cincinnati. He spent some time on the docks around the *Hilde.*"

Simon's eyes sparked. "This is most interesting. May I speak with him?"

"Yes, of course. But you won't frighten him, will you? I want to help Luke, but Clay's only a child."

Simon rose from his chair, closing the short distance between them. His clean, toilet water scent wafted about her as he stooped and took her hand. "Miss Larson," he assured, "I don't wish to harm the boy. I will be as sympathetic as I can, but I must pursue every lead that might help Luke."

"Very well." Claire rose.

"Oh, Miss Larson?"

"Yes."

"Where is Davy?"

"He's taking his nap," she replied. "I'll be just a minute."

Claire left the room and returned with a ten year old who studied Simon with suspicious blue eyes from atop a freckled nose. She introduced the two and Clay relaxed after Simon's friendly handshake. Claire issued a small sigh of relief, then snuggled in close to the child on a frayed settee.

Simon cleared his throat. "Clay, I understand that you have had some hard times. I know the people here, the Murdocks and Miss Larson. They'll take good care of you from now on. They're kind folks. I'm Miss Larson's friend, and I want to help another one of her friends, Davy's father."

The boy smiled. "Davy's a good baby," he said.

Simon chuckled. "Yes, he is. Now, Clay, I want you to know that you can trust me. Do you understand?"

"I think so. You want me to help Davy's pa?"

Simon's nod was slow and nonthreatening. "That's right. Just tell me what you saw on the docks."

Clay cast anxious eyes at Claire, who nodded her assent, and the youngster began to talk. "I was on the docks long enough to get to know most of the rigs. I stowed away on the *Barnacle*." He glanced at Simon to see his reaction. Simon smiled and waited.

"You sure I won't get in trouble?"

"I promise."

Then the child surprised Simon with his cliff-edged abruptness. "I saw Mr. Gates kill a man and throw him overboard."

Simon scooted to the very edge of his seat, every nerve quickened. "How did he kill him?"

"Hit him."

"Do you know who the man was?"

"Farthington," said Clay.

"Silas Farthington?"

"Yes, Sir." Clay's eyes lit.

From his investigative research, the name rang familiar. "He had worked for Aaron Gates. Do you know why this happened?"

"No, Sir. They were arguing. Mr. Gates was angry . . . and drunk."

"Where were you when you saw this?"

"Down on the docks, loading fish."

"Was there anyone else with Mr. Gates and Silas?"

Clay nodded furiously, and Simon knew in that instant that the boy spoke truthfully. "Gates's son, Ruben, was with him."

"Ruben! Well, I'll be. Anyone else?"

"Yup, but I don't know that one's name."

"Would you recognize him if you saw him again?"

Claire's upward glance was protective and questioning, causing Simon to quickly dispel any thoughts he might have of dragging this child back onto the docks. Nevertheless, Clay answered his question. "I only saw the old man around the docks a couple times. I don't know his name. He looked like an old grizzly bear."

"Thank you, Clay." Simon mentally noted the description. "I'm sure this information will benefit Davy's pa." He reached toward the lad and shook his hand. "You're a brave boy."

"Thank ya, Mr. Appleby."

"You may go now, Clay," Claire said, sending the boy off with a hug.

"Whew." Simon exhaled a long, wheezy breath after the boy was gone. "This is exactly the kind of breakthrough I've been looking for. Maybe now I can get to the bottom of this case. Thank you, Miss Larson."

Simon jumped to his feet with great enthusiasm, and Claire escorted him to the door. She stood there long after the chestnut bay led Simon's carriage out of sight, wondering, hoping, when a tiny hand slipped into her own. "Miss Claire," a small voice pleaded. She smiled down at the child, turning back to the task at hand.

The door creaked, moaned, and slammed, making its now familiar reverberations; then footsteps clacked, abating until Sheriff Watson disappeared.

"Hello, Luke!" Simon greeted.

"Hello yourself." Luke cocked his head. "You sound extra cheerful today."

"I am." Simon squatted onto the small stool provided. "We've hit upon some new information."

Luke listened intently as Simon retold the orphan's eyewitness account of Silas Farthington's murder. Afterward he rubbed his chin. "Hmm? What do you make of it, Simon?"

"The child was obviously telling the truth, so I paid the Gateses another visit. Ruben denied everything, which comes as no surprise. He said it was just a case of drowning, that I could check the newspaper. I'm certain he's lying." Simon's face reflected distaste as he added, "I also looked up a seedy character I came across at the docks. I think he is somehow involved. Name is Clancy. He could very well be Clay's 'old man.' Supposedly, Clancy bought the *Hilde* from Ruben, but I believe there's more to it than that."

"What did he say?"

Simon snorted. "Clancy? He just laughed uproariously and spit tobacco juice at my boots."

A sigh of disappointment escaped Luke's lips, followed by another question. "I wonder what Aaron Gates was involved in?"

"So do I. And how is Ruben connected? He split from his pa about the time Farthington was found dead. Moved away."

Luke tugged at his mustache thoughtfully. "But he showed up again when Aaron died?"

Simon nodded. "Whatever it is, Ruth must be in on it, to fix the blame on you so hastily. I thought it might be a lover, but now I seriously doubt it, especially if Clancy is involved." Simon chuckled, then stood, rubbed his palms together, and paced in a semicircle. "I need to turn over some rocks."

Luke remained seated while Simon deliberated. "I just wish we had more time," the lawyer issued with vehemence. "These loose ends won't do us any good as they are."

"Can't the boy testify?"

"He could, but Claire wants to protect him. Truth is the jury probably wouldn't believe him anyway. The defense would cut him to shreds with his background, and he's too vulnerable for that right now."

"I understand."

Simon adjusted his necktie and recovered his hat. "I'd better be off now, to do some more digging. I think I'll look up Mrs. Farthington today."

"Simon, before you go . . ." The lawyer turned his attention back to Luke, eyes questioning. "My father arrived. He's got time on his hands. Is there anything he can do to help you?"

"Is he up to it?"

Luke laughed. "And then some."

"Where's he staying?"

"At the Trader's Inn."

"Good. I'll look him up."

"Simon, by the way, he's a preacher."

"Another preacher!" Simon rolled his eyes in a teasing manner, and Luke laughed.

CHAPTER 6

During the two weeks that had passed since Luke's arrest, his emotions wavered between the confidence that truth would prevail and the full-blown hopelessness that he would never be free again. Though his emotions fluctuated, his deep-seated faith did not. He discovered that his heavenly Father provided him with ample portions of faith — enough to endure each day's trials.

This particular morning Luke agonized upon bent knee. "Jesus, they took You like a lamb to the slaughter, and You went willingly though You knew what awaited." Sorrow filled Luke's spirit, and he sobbed, his chest heaving from brokenness. "Yet You were innocent. Oh, Lord, please restore my faith. Prepare me for my destiny."

From where Luke knelt by his cot, he buried his head in his arms, weeping as he waited upon God. He felt so weak, and today was his trial.

At eight o'clock that morning, Sheriff Watson ushered Luke down the center aisle of the two-story brick courthouse to occupy his place at the front. A swelling peace within Luke's breast assured him of God's presence.

As he passed, a murmur sifted throughout the crowded courtroom. The faces of parishioners and friends conveyed grief-stricken expressions. Many curious stares dotted the throng of spectators. Some even cast sympathetic glances across the room to the widow Gates and her children.

Directly behind the Gates family, Uriah Cook sat with his wife, Emma. The widow's key witness — arms folded across his chest — wore an expression much like a cat with a plump mouse. Emma, however, sat rigid with lips pressed tight together and clasped hands turning her fingers unnaturally white.

Across the courtroom behind Luke, Rev. Emmett Wheeler observed Simon as he leaned sideways to whisper something in his son's ear. Emmett silently prayed for a miracle. As Simon's errand boy over the last several days, he knew the lawyer's case was weak, revolving around assumptions that contained numerous loose ends. He did not fault the man, however, for Emmett had experienced firsthand the lawyer's fervent efforts to solve Luke's case.

Now he watched as Luke gave his lawyer a weak grin. "I trust you, Simon. You and God."

"I wish you wouldn't put me on the same level as God," Simon protested from the corner of his mouth.

"I'm not. I just believe you are His hands in this."

A slamming of the gavel silenced the whispers, and Judge Francis Dunlevy cleared his throat. Emmett Wheeler leaned forward to press his son's shoulder as the judge opened the trial. "The Common Pleas Court of Dayton will now convene to hear the case of *Gates v. Wheeler.* On my left is the plaintiff, Ruth Gates, represented by Edmund Fulton, and on my right is the defendant, Rev. Luke Wheeler, represented by Simon Appleby. Prosecutor Fulton, you may begin."

"My first witness, Your Honor, is Ruth Gates, widow of the murder victim."

The woman at the witness stand fingered the white handkerchief, sheer and lacy, which lay in contrast against the skirt of her dark mourning gown. Equally so, her delicate flawless face made a striking statement framed in the widow's black. The dark beauty's deep brown eyes moved those in the courtroom like the strains of a sad melody, evoking heartfelt sympathy. Ruth Gates raised her dusky gaze full into the face of Edmund Fulton, who now questioned her.

Pacing back and forth, he tread an invisible path seven feet in length. "How exactly did Luke Wheeler respond when you expressed your condolences over his wife's death?"

She answered as rehearsed, "His eyes went glassy, like his soul left his body. Then they fixed on me, and he came at me like a sleepwalker. I was so frightened that I backed up against the stove. I remember knocking some pots off." She twisted the handkerchief. "I was trapped, and he kept coming."

"Did he say anything to you during this time?"

"Yes, he kept calling me Miriam."

"Are you saying Luke Wheeler thought you were his wife?"

Ruth nodded her black-bonneted head emphatically. Leaning forward, Judge Dunlevy gently admonished her, "Please answer Mr. Fulton audibly, Mrs. Gates, so the jury can hear."

"Oh, sorry, Your Honor. Yes. The preacher was acting crazy."

A murmur spread throughout the courtroom.

"What happened after he pinned you to the stove?"

"He tried to kiss me. I screamed, and he hit me." Ruth gingerly touched her handkerchief to her face as if it still ached. "Aaron heard me and ran to the house, where he tore the preacher off me. They struggled, and the preacher knocked Aaron down. He hit his head. The preacher killed him."

"What happened after Aaron fell to the floor?"

Ruth dabbed her eyes before she answered. "He wasn't breathing."

Edmund Fulton's spindly legs whisked to her side.

"I know this is hard, Mrs. Gates. Please, take your time." He raked steely, accusing eyes across Luke.

Luke's red face blanched, and he whispered a silent prayer.

"The preacher begged me to forgive him," Ruth Gates continued. "He gripped my arms so tight they bruised."

Fulton leaned close. "Go on."

"Why, then Uriah came and saved me. Didn't you, Uriah?"

"Shore did!" the man piped up from his seat.

The silver-haired judge glared at Uriah Cook for a moment, then pointed his finger at him. "You, Sir, are not the one on the stand and will remain quiet," he scolded. He transposed his stare onto Fulton, as if faulting him for the disruption.

"That is all, Your Honor," Fulton said with a contrite bow of his head.

Next Luke was summoned to the stand. Edmund Fulton paced, swinging equally elongated legs and arms, then stopped suddenly — a ploy he used to gain the full attention of the courtroom. Expectantly, the crowd hushed immediately in breath-holding suspense. Several people leaned forward in their seats.

"Mr. Wheeler, how long has it been since your wife's death?"

Luke's eyes, windows of pain and sorrow, met Fulton's accusing ones. "Almost three months, Sir."

"Is it true that you loved your wife and deeply grieved her death?"

Luke set his jaw and concentrated on his answer. "Yes, of course."

"Were you acquainted with Ruth Gates before the day of the crime?"

Luke glanced over the crowd, his gaze resting upon the front bench where Ruth Gates sat. In vain he searched her face for some sign of penitence. But her expression remained stony. "Yes," he answered.

"How?"

"She attended my church on occasion."

"Isn't it true that most folks see a resemblance between Ruth Gates and your late wife?"

Calmly Luke answered, "I've heard some do, but personally I don't see it. Mrs. Gates is much older, and her countenance much harder."

Simon stifled a grin at Ruth's gasp of insult, and her lawyer's consequent frown. But Fulton recovered with practiced speed. "So," he said, "you acknowledge that there is a resemblance."

"Yes."

"Were you acquainted with Aaron Gates as well?"

Luke answered, "Yes."

"What were you doing at their home the afternoon of the crime?"

"I went to fulfill a promise to my wife, Miriam."

Luke's answer was an unexpected twist, one which pleased Fulton. The prosecutor's face lit with apperception as he shrewdly abandoned his previously intended line of questioning. Carefully, he stalked his prey. "So your thoughts were preoccupied with

Miriam that day?"

Luke conceded. "In a way."

Then Fulton pounced on Luke like a tiger. "Considering your blinding grief and Miriam's resemblance to Ruth Gates, is it possible you mistook Ruth for Miriam?"

Refusal played across Luke's face. "No!"

"Did you strike Ruth when she would not allow you to kiss her?"

"No!" Luke looked to Simon with a silent plea for help.

His lawyer did not respond, though his face indicated grave displeasure at the way Edmund Fulton was attempting to use this — Dayton's first murder trial — to make a name for himself.

Fulton asked, "Isn't it true that Aaron Gates repeatedly warned you to stay away from his wife?"

"What?"

"I understand, Mr. Wheeler, it is hard for you to concentrate in your unstable condition. . . ."

"Objection, Your Honor." Simon leapt to his feet.

"Sustained. Restate your question, Prosecutor."

"Had Aaron Gates warned you to stay away from his wife?"

"Well, yes, but he was drunk at the time.

He had no grounds to —"

Fulton interrupted. "What exactly did he say to you?"

Luke grappled for an answer that was not self-incriminating. When he hesitated, Fulton pressed. "I understand there was a public disturbance with witnesses. Shall I call Mrs. Gates back to the stand?"

Luke's shoulders slumped as he mumbled, "He said to stay away from Ruth."

"I'm sorry, could you speak up?"

Luke repeated, "He said to stay away from Ruth."

"That is all. I have no further questions."

Simon Appleby's sweeping gaze stole across the stuffy, overcrowded courtroom, cognizant of those who relied on him — Luke, Emmett Wheeler, Claire, Luke's parishioners and friends. If only he had a stronger case. Nevertheless, after giving his client an encouraging smile, he began to question him.

"Reverend, what did you hear as you approached the Gates home?"

Luke answered with conviction, "I heard two men and Mrs. Gates arguing inside the house."

"Did you enter the house?"

"Yes, because Ruth Gates screamed, a hideous scream. I rushed inside to help."

"What did you find?"

"Aaron Gates lay on the floor bleeding, Ruth Gates bent over him."

Simon paused to allow the jury to visualize this scene before continuing his interrogation. "Where was the third person?"

"Gone out the kitchen window," Luke answered. "It was open, and the curtain was half ripped off the wall. Other nearby items were knocked about. And I heard his horse ride off."

The crowd gasped. Pleased with this response, Simon asked, "What happened after that?"

"I placed my hanky around Aaron Gates's head to stop the bleeding, but he died in my arms. Ruth begged me to help. That was when I noticed her swollen face." Luke's own face dripped of perspiration, which he wiped away with his hand as he continued. "The smell of liquor oozed from Aaron Gates's body, and I assumed he'd hit his wife. Naturally, I tried to console her as I would any sister in my congregation."

Simon urged, "Go on."

"Ruth grew calmer until Uriah came. That's when she turned on me. She made up things to frame me and protect whoever went out that window."

"Thank you. That will be all for now."

As Luke returned to his seat in the front of the packed courtroom, the spectators used the opportunity to stir from their uncomfortable positions. Men wiped their brows and swatted at flies while women tugged at sticky skirts, many fanning their faces.

Simon rearranged his tight necktie and proceeded to call Ruth Gates to the stand. He recaptured the crowd's attention with his sharp questions, like zipping, burning arrows.

"Mrs. Gates, why did you threaten me when I examined the ground outside your house?"

Ruth stammered, "Y–you scared the children. They'd been through enough. I–I just wanted you to leave."

Simon flinched at the mention of her children. This could sway the jury. Against his better judgment, however, he continued with this barbed method of interrogation to pursue the issue.

"Upon examination, I noticed the ground was freshly raked around the outside of the kitchen window, the window which Rev. Wheeler testified was used as an escape route. Mrs. Gates, were you trying to cover someone's tracks?"

"Objection! The witness is not on trial

here," Fulton reminded the judge.

"Overruled. Answer the question, please, Mrs. Gates."

Fulton dropped back into his seat.

She thrust her chin upward. "I don't know what you're talking about. I never did such a thing."

Simon played on a hunch. "Were you, in fact, trying to protect your own son, Ruben?"

"No! I was not!" Ruth jumped to her feet. "That man!" She pointed to Luke. "He killed my husband. I saw it with my own eyes, and you're just trying to get him off the hook!"

In response, someone from within the group of spectators yelled, "What weapon did the preacher use? His Bible?"

An outburst of laughter instantly filled the room while the judge's cheeks turned red as July's tomatoes. With white eyebrows poised in consternation, he banged his gavel repeatedly until order was restored.

Simon changed tactics. "Mrs. Gates, if Rev. Wheeler's story is not true, how did his hanky get on your husband's head?"

She shook her head adamantly. "There was no hanky. The preacher's a liar. He made that up, too."

Aware that Ruth's testimony was harming

their case and generating undue sympathy, Simon dismissed her to call Uriah Cook as his next witness.

Once Uriah was settled, Simon addressed him. "Mr. Cook, was there a hanky on Aaron Gates's head?"

"No, Sir. I never saw one."

Eyes widened through the courtroom. Luke lunged forward, restrained only by his father's firm grip upon his shoulder.

Simon stared at the witness in disbelief, now wondering what part Uriah played in this deception. Was he the accomplice? Uriah began to squirm under Simon's intense scrutiny.

"Do you know the penalty for perjury?"

"Yes, Sir," Uriah said. "Like I said, there was no hanky. The preacher lied." He gestured toward Ruth. "Everything Ruth Gates says is true. Why, I saw the way the preacher was mishandling her!"

Simon approached the judge. "Your Honor, this deception is much more wide-spread than I had anticipated. I ask for a recess. I believe I can prove —"

His appeal upset Judge Dunlevy, whose duties included riding circuit, and his departure had already been postponed for this case. Those responsibilities weighed heavily upon him now. "No recess, Barrister

Appleby. You should have done your home-work."

As Simon wheeled away from the bench, he noticed a pair of leering eyes from the back of the courtroom — Clancy from the docks. The unscrupulous fisherman laughed out loud, as if taking pleasure in the fact that his presence further rankled the fancy lawyer.

The sweltering days that followed wore grim and long as piece by piece Luke's case was decimated. In the end, one of the testimonies that swayed the jury was that of Sheriff Watson.

"No, Sir," he had replied, "there was no hanky when I got there." Furthermore, he destroyed Luke with his closing remark. "After being around the reverend these past weeks, I find it hard to believe he could have killed anybody. Of course he was like a crazy man when I first locked him up."

On the fifth day of the trial, July 8, the afternoon hours waned as the attorneys delivered their concluding statements. Subsequently, the jury deliberated in the upper story of the small brick courthouse for about an hour. Upon their return Judge Dunlevy heard the verdict and swiftly announced his sentence.

"This court finds Luke Wheeler guilty of murder. I hereby sentence him to hang by the neck until dead, the day after tomorrow at noon."

Claire flew to her feet and screamed, "No! No!"

Equally stunned, Mary Anders clasped hold of the anguished woman's shoulders, easing her back onto the bench where she and Gustaf attended to her.

At the decree, the room buzzed with heated discussion and Luke's world spun madly. He collapsed in his seat, oblivious of those about him just before the blackness came. The stinging, he realized, was Simon patting his cheeks to revive him. Sheriff Watson allowed Simon and Emmett to support Luke as he propelled them through the crowd — which hushed as they passed — back to his cell.

CHAPTER 7

The hoofs of Simon's chestnut bay beat against summer's parched road to the Gates home. *That woman bewitched the jury. She has to have an Achilles' heel. If only I could prove —* Simon ducked his hat-clad head just in time to avoid the sharp claws of an overhanging limb. "Easy, Boy," he soothed and slowed their pace.

A mile and a half later, he dismounted and approached the Gateses' dwelling with apprehension. The place reeked of foul play. The air felt suffocating, the shadows menacing. He removed his hat, drew in a deep breath of the virulent atmosphere, and knocked. After days of courtroom interrogations, the widow Gates's beauty still shocked him. He tapped his hat against his leg. "Mrs. Gates."

"What do you want? The trial's over." Simon thrust his right leg inside. The weight of the door's heavy impact crushed upon him, causing him to stagger backwards. However, he recovered enough to shoulder the gaping door open and push his way inside.

She backed up. Her hateful glare met his smoldering one.

She was the first to relent. "What do you want?"

"An innocent man is going to hang. His blood, as well as Aaron's, will be on your hands for eternity."

Ruth's face flinched, her voice hard. "Is that all?"

"When the truth eventually comes out, you may hang. Are you willing to die for the one you protect?"

Before she could reply, a cry rang out. "Mama!" Young Tom Gates burst through the open doorway, then stopped when he recognized Simon.

Ruth jerked her head. "In a minute, Tommy. We have a visitor who will soon be leaving. Run along now." She motioned for him to leave.

"Yes, Ma'am," the boy mumbled, but he hesitated, allowing Simon just enough time to notice the shiny object that the boy fingered nervously.

"Tom! Wait!" he called out before Tom fled from the room. "What a fine knife you have there! Can I see it?" Pride swallowed up the boy's better judgment, and he thrust it out for Simon's inspection.

Ruth's eyes narrowed in distrust. As the lawyer palmed the metal object, he complimented the boy again. "Yes, mighty fine. Don't recall when I've seen such a nice piece. Where'd you get it?"

"My brother Ruben gave it to me the day —" Tom broke midsentence, catching his mistake upon remembering Simon's appearance at the docks.

The lad's desire to hide the fact that Ruben was in Dayton corroborated Simon's hunch from the first day of the trial: Ruben must be involved. Perhaps he was the one who had fled through the open window.

"Oh, yes," Simon said, "I remember seeing you on the docks that day, coming off the *Hilde.* Here, Son." He returned the knife, and Tom dashed for the door.

Slowly, Simon turned to Ruth with a fortitude that unsettled her. "You realize, of course, it will only be a matter of time until I can prove that Ruben was in Dayton all along, that Aaron killed Silas Farthington, and you are an accomplice to your husband's murder. It would be much better for you if you came forward with the truth now."

Ruth's eyes widened, but her lips remained clenched in a straight, fine line, determined to seal off the truth. Simon tried one last tactic, an appeal to a mother's heart. "Remember, not only is Luke Wheeler a man of God, but he is also a widower and father of a small baby. That little boy needs him. Surely, you cannot allow his father to die."

"Leave now, Mr. Appleby!"

Simon looked at her unflinching face. "You'll regret this until your dying day," he said with loathing.

"Is that a threat?"

"Of course not! Just the hard truth." Deeply frustrated, he wheeled and left.

Luke stared out the small barred window, watching the carpenters. The sound of hammers broke the otherwise eerie quiet. The sweet smell of sawdust mixed with the more repugnant odors of dust and sweat, permeating through the open window. *Where is justice?* he wondered as he listened to the scraping of lumber, creaking of boards, and thunder of hammers driving nails into the gallows.

Thus Simon caught him unawares, gazing into the distant space, when he came to visit. Startled out of his vacant stare, Luke asked him forthrightly, "What does a man do when he knows he has but hours to live?"

Simon straddled the wooden stool in Luke's cell and considered the legitimate question. "Tie up loose ends, I guess, make things right, say his good-byes."

"My relationships are all in order — I'm ready to meet my Lord. I've even forgiven Ruth. I know she wouldn't do this if she wasn't hurting in some way."

Simon nodded, not intending to tell Luke of his visit that morning since nothing good came of it.

Luke continued, "Mostly I concentrate on meeting Jesus and seeing Miriam again. That gives me strength. But it just doesn't seem possible that one minute I can be in this miserable cell, and the next walking on golden streets in eternity, does it?"

Simon shook his head. He certainly could not comprehend it. He could not visualize this man's life snuffed. He shuddered.

"What about the good-byes? Is there anyone you want to see yet?"

"Father's gone to bring Claire and Davy over for awhile. Then he's going to stay with me 'til the end."

"Well, I'll stay here if you like until he returns."

"That would be kind of you. And, Simon,

thank you for trying. I know this is not easy for you. You did your best. Don't blame yourself. It must be God's plan for me, to bring me home."

"I wish I could have done more." Simon hung his head.

When Emmett Wheeler returned alone, Simon and Luke looked at him questioningly. He answered their unspoken inquiry. "Claire will be over later; Davy was asleep."

Rising to take his leave, Simon grasped the prisoner by the shoulders, pulling him into a wordless embrace. "I'll be here in the morning. Be strong, Luke," he said in a low tone.

"Thank you, Simon."

Luke watched his friend disappear, then gave a start when his father grabbed his shoulder, turning him about.

"What is it, Father?"

Emmett leaned close to whisper, his face aglow. "There's a plan, Luke!"

"What do you mean?"

"Ssh! Come listen." Again Emmett whispered excitedly, "A plan for your escape!"

"But, Father," Luke argued, "I'm not a coward! This can't be the Christian way."

Emmett placed a weary hand upon his son's shoulder and tried once more to convince him. "Christ eluded the angry mobs."

Dubious, yet wanting desperately to believe his father, Luke grappled with the issue. Was it an acceptable option? Could there be any honor, any scruples in such a thing?

His father reasoned, "Oh, all right. It's not quite the same." His voice raised. "But you're innocent, and to hang isn't justifiable either."

Luke's will to survive, along with his father's pleading, finally persuaded him. With a nod, he conceded, "You're right, Father. If this is the Lord's plan for my life — to escape — I must try it."

"That's my boy," Emmett whispered with relief. "Quickly now, we must go over the details. There's much to be done."

The plan began when Gustaf arrived at the jail shortly before dark. As usual, Sheriff Watson accompanied him to Luke's cell, but when he turned to leave, Luke detained him with a question. "Sheriff?"

Curious, Sheriff Watson turned back toward the condemned one. "Yeah?"

Luke's hands gripped the iron bars, and from where his face was pressed between them, he glanced at the metal lock. "Could you bend the rules a bit? I could really use the support right now."

Sheriff Watson sympathized with Luke. "Guess that won't harm anybody." The sheriff despised this part of his job — attending a prisoner facing death. He twisted the key and waited for Gustaf to enter the cell with Emmett and Luke. With the special privileges allotted a clergyman, Emmett was already inside the cell.

Upon returning to his outer office, Sheriff Watson heard a disturbance out front and hurried to the window to investigate. "Aw, no!" he muttered and fumbled for his hat and rifle, then swung the door open and stood in its wake, his weapon ready. The group gathered outside were many of Luke's parishioners. "You folks need to disassemble!" the sheriff warned them.

"We won't let you hang the preacher," one man shouted heatedly.

"Now listen, you men know the law is the law!"

Meanwhile the three inside Luke's cell scrambled to receive items that were being passed to them through the barred window. Outside, Jesse Murdock, one of Luke's parishioners, poked two small cloth pouches filled with hearth ashes along with a tiny container of tree sap through the tight bars.

Then Gustaf drew two bedsheets into the room and swiftly shoved them beneath Luke's cot.

Emmett grabbed the razor that appeared next. "God bless you, Jesse."

"May God be with you, Luke," Jesse whispered back hoarsely. Then after careful surveillance in all directions, he disappeared.

Gustaf motioned at Luke. "You do it, my hand's too shaky."

Luke grinned. "All right. Father, let's see what you look like beneath that beard." Knowing every second accounted for precious time, Luke made quick even strokes across his father's face, and the man's beard vanished, revealing a squarish, shocking-white chin. Gustaf brushed the small, white curls onto a neat pile for reuse, to be pasted upon Luke's own chin later.

Fastidiously, the men worked over Luke to concoct a clever disguise. First, the Wheelers exchanged clothing. Next, Emmett powdered his son's yellow hair with the hearth ashes until it appeared as gray as his own. Gustaf applied a generous amount of tree sap to Luke's chin, then neatly attached Emmett's shavings, patting and designing a nice beard for him. With satisfaction, all remaining traces of the caper were concealed beneath Luke's cot.

When the time was right and the crowd outside had dispersed, Gustaf called out to Sheriff Watson. "Ready to leave now, Sheriff!"

The lawman arrived, looking haggard from his riotous encounter. On cue, Gustaf began the charade.

"I'm gonna take Emmett to get a bite to eat and give Luke a moment alone." Sheriff Watson cast a glance at the man on the cot with a Bible stuck in his face, presuming that one was his prisoner, and nodded. As they left the cell, Luke used Gustaf as a shield as the older man diverted the sheriff's attention with small talk.

Once outside on Main Street, both men heard the heavy door slam and the latch being locked on the inside. Gustaf whispered, "I see the sheriff isn't going to take any chances of losing his prisoner to a mob." Luke emitted a nervous chuckle at the irony of the situation as they hurried to the place where his horse awaited, saddled.

"Claire'll meet you at King's Ferry with Davy."

"What?" Luke clearly did not want to involve them in any danger.

Gustaf shrugged. "You know Claire. She thought you would want to say good-bye to the child." At Luke's displeasure, he contin-ued, "She would not take 'no' for an an-swer." He gave Luke a small push. "Now go. And God be with you."

The two men embraced before Luke scaled his spirited brown mount and headed for the river, propelled forward by a steady supply of adrenaline pumping through his veins.

Darkness fell across the Miami River in deepening shades of gray. Luke expelled a trembling sigh of relief; he had reached the ferry in the nick of time before its final daily excursion. He paused to consider the many minute details his friends had coordinated to accomplish this escape. But there was no time for sentimentality. Casting the thought aside, he dismounted and scanned the area, but he did not see Claire. Just as well.

Quickly, he approached the two dark, siz-able figures that seemed to be in charge of the ferry. "Room for me and my horse?" Luke inquired.

"Twelve and one-half cents!" one man said, then spit tobacco juice into the water.

With trepidation, Luke rummaged through his father's trousers pocket. He was relieved to feel a lump of money most certainly put there intentionally. Withdrawing a small portion, he counted out the fee to the spitter with the red bandanna and dark beard.

The planks of the sloping ramp creaked like an old barn door as Luke coaxed his skittish horse to board the river ferry, which was secured with cables between the east and west shores. Once this was accomplished, he murmured gently to his frightened beast, tethering her to a hitching post near the center of the floating barge.

Luke's eyes searched the dimly lit ferry. He faintly discerned the silhouette of a skirt. It appeared to be the only female passenger among the group. Surely Claire wouldn't have boarded the ferry. He started toward her. "Claire?"

"Luke? Is that you?" Claire giggled tearfully when she was able to make out his features. "You look so funny."

"Come over here by the railing," he whispered. After putting distance between themselves and the other passengers, Luke drew both her and Davy into his arms. "I can't believe this is happening," he whispered against her hair.

"I was so frightened."

"You poor thing. Why did you come aboard? You should not have come at all."

"Not for me, for you. I was afraid you

might be killed or wounded, lying some-where bleeding —"

"Ssh. I'm fine, as you can see." He released her, holding up his arms for her to inspect his person.

Claire wiped her tears away with a free hand and giggled again at the sight of him and his haphazard beard. Knowing their time for good-byes was short, she offered Davy. With the baby in his arms, Luke turned his back to the others aboard and gazed out over the dark water, its choppy surface now barely visible since the stars were not yet shining.

Luke managed to calm his still-thundering heart enough to speak soft endearments to Davy who, in turn, struggled against his father's chest with screaming protest. "Davy, my son. Have you missed your pa?" The baby calmed and eventually quit squirming at the familiar voice. Unexpectedly, Davy swiped chubby fingers across his beard, whacking off a portion of whiskers. "Hey! I'll need those just awhile longer." Luke laughed. He pried the boy's fist open and brushed away the loose stubbles as he turned to Claire.

Before he could speak, however, the barge lurched violently, knocking them both off balance. Claire grabbed for the railing and held tight. Then they were adrift with two men poling the ferry and a strong breeze brushing across their faces. "You all right?" he asked her.

"Yes." She nodded.

"You were supposed to get off before we launched! Maybe I can stop them!"

Claire grabbed Luke's sleeve. "No! Don't cause a scene. That wouldn't be good for your situation."

Panicking, Luke's voice raised. "But what will you do now?"

Blurting the first thing that came to her mind, Claire said, "Just ride the ferry back across. Don't worry."

"But I am worried!"

"Sh! Not so loud," Claire cautioned.

"But you're the only woman aboard." Luke leaned close to confide, "I've never seen the pair handling this ferry before. King must have hired some new men. I don't feel good about this, Claire."

"Maybe more folks will join us on the other shore."

"We'll see," Luke replied skeptically. Not wanting to spend these final moments arguing, he dropped the issue. "Claire?"

"Yes."

Touching her shoulder, he said, "Thanks for coming and for everything you've done for me these past weeks. Father's agreed to take Davy back to Ben in Beaver Creek. When I'm free again, I'll go to him there."

Claire smiled, looking up into his eyes. "I thought as much. And I'm confident you will be free soon."

Luke shifted his touch to her elbow, guiding her to a nearby bench, and they settled in for the remainder of the passage. Half an hour passed in which Luke played with Davy. When they approached the docks of the opposite shore, he reluctantly gave up the child, and at Claire's insistence . . . he finally left them.

However, once aground, he tethered his horse close to the ferry and positioned himself in the shadows. His intention was to watch those boarding, keeping an eye out for Claire and Davy's safety until they were adrift again.

To watch them huddled together in the spot where he had left them was excruciating. An icy loneliness gripped him. What choice had he? Being on the run, he did not know what dangers to expect. He shivered uncontrollably, wishing some women or children would board. But they did not, and worse still, the bearded man with the red bandanna was even now approaching Claire.

"No place to go, Ma'am?" the man asked.

Luke strained but could not hear her reply. But he heard the man's coarse laughter and vulgar response. "I won't mind keeping you company on the long ride home."

Luke muttered under his breath as he bolted back toward the ferry. His boots clacking on the wood-bottomed barge caused such a commotion as to startle Claire and her antagonist. When they turned toward him, Luke blurted out the first thing that came to his mind, "Come on, Claire! We must hurry!" He grabbed Claire's arm to lead her and Davy away, but the bearded one was not to be easily discouraged. He followed and spun Luke around.

"What's the hurry? The lady and me was having a talk, weren't we, Honey?"

"No! We were not!" Claire snapped.

The man then took a swing at Luke, barely grazing his chin, swiping off a fistful of fuzz. "Well, what've we got here? An impostor?" He let out a whoop. "Pretty frisky for an old feller."

Luke hollered, "Run, Claire! Get the horse!" Claire flew with Davy, and Luke found himself facing the offender. The man narrowed his eyes. "What're you up to? You got a reward on your head?"

Unexpectedly, the man lunged at Luke, but Luke dodged him with catlike swiftness, at the same time releasing a sidelong swing that connected soundly with the man's neck. The strike was powerful — pumping adrenaline had maximized Luke's strength far beyond his usual ability — and the man reeled just long enough for Luke to make his escape.

Claire never knew exactly what happened, but by the time she had fetched Luke's horse, Luke was beside her, breathless. Then he was mounted and pulling her up behind him. "Hold on," he hollered, and they galloped off with Davy sandwiched between them, fast leaving the ferry behind.

Meanwhile back at the jail, Deputy Galloway had come to relieve Sheriff Watson for the nighttime shift, just as usual. This was what Emmett had been waiting for. Now it was time to finish this ploy. "Deputy!"

The lawman soon appeared, and Emmett whispered, "My son fell asleep." He rubbed his chin with his huge hand, trying to cover the smooth white area where his beard had once been. At the same time, he pointed to the cot where a lump resembling a man's form — the sheets that had been pulled through the bars — was visible beneath the wool blanket. "Do you mind if I leave for awhile and get a bite to eat?"

"Sure, Reverend," the deputy whispered back. "I'm surprised he can sleep." As Galloway eyed the lump, Emmett walked past him and out of the jailhouse. Exhaling a sigh of relief, he looked heavenward. "Thank You, Lord."

Remembering something, he changed directions and passed beneath the small barred window. He stooped to pick up the items that had been previously flung out the window. Grimly, Emmett stared at the looming gallows before him.

He bowed his head. "Lord, forgive me for this falsehood," he breathed. Lifting his head, he tucked the bundle beneath his arm, turned his back to the ugly structure with its poignant smell of death, and rushed toward his hotel.

CHAPTER 8

A remote Indian trail sliced across the Mad River Road, penetrating a heavily wooded area. Here Luke veered east, considerably slowing their previously furious gait to forge untamed forest. Not far within this timberland's tangle of decaying tree stumps, strewn logs, and hock-crippling gorges lay a tiny cove where the near-full moon now cast a welcomed glow.

Upon discovering this secluded haven, he slid from the saddle and helped Claire and Davy dismount. Still winded from their narrow escape at King's Ferry, Luke shook his head. "That was a close call! I'm sorry, Claire. I sure didn't intend to drag you and Davy into this."

He slapped off his hat with one hand and ran his other through his ash-powdered hair, raising a smoky cloud that made him cough. "What a mess I've gotten us into!" He yanked his hat back onto his head and began to pace.

Claire's hairpins had fallen out by now, and her hair hung long and wild. She brushed it off her face as best she could, but Davy's pink fist flew up and latched onto a strand. Claire planted a wet kiss on the baby's cheek and ventured, "Luke?"

He stopped his pacing and faced her wordlessly, several feet away.

"It's not your fault" — she motioned wide with her arm — "any of this. The important thing is that you are free and alive. You must not abort your plans because of us. I can ride. See? I even wore my riding skirt."

Luke went to her where she stood clutching her skirt and lightly touched her arm. "Claire, I need to think. Why don't you have a seat over there on that stump and take a rest?"

Claire nodded and settled herself, rocking Davy gently while she rummaged through the baby's pouch. She diapered him, then withdrew a small bottle of milk. Luke watched as the baby sucked hungrily at first, then more rhythmically, and finally started to nod off.

"Do you have much food along for Davy?"

Claire whispered, "Enough to last through the night."

"When you're rested, we'll start toward

Beaver Creek. I'm to make a rendezvous with some men coming our way. Arrangements have been made to exchange mounts to confuse the law, put them onto a false trail."

"I know."

Luke's startled look caused Claire to explain. "According to Gustaf, this plan was in place for quite awhile. As soon as the verdict was announced, riders were sent to Beaver Creek to make arrangements."

Shaking his head, Luke said, "You don't know how humbled I am, how touched I feel. . . ." His voice faded.

After several moments, he continued, "When we meet up with the riders from Beaver Creek, you and Davy can go with them."

"No!" Claire cringed at the thought of consorting with perfect strangers. Luke swung around and looked at her in astonishment. Her tone had disturbed Davy's slumber. "Please," she begged while rocking the child, "let me stay with you."

"We'll see," he said gently. "But for now, the more miles we put behind us, the better."

Luke recalled that Gustaf mentioned supplies being packed and hoped no one had removed his personal articles normally stashed there. With relief, he withdrew an object made of cloth and leather. Holding the contraption out for Claire's inspection, he said, "A sling for Davy. Would you like me to carry him?"

Claire scrambled to her feet. "I believe I can manage with the help of that sling. Why don't you let me try?"

Luke smiled. "All right. Come here and let me show you how this works." Carefully he reached one arm around Claire while placing the sling beneath the sleeping baby's rump and back. Then gingerly he turned Claire around so he could secure the buckle at her waist and across her back. "Comfortable?" he asked with a mischievous grin.

Claire returned his smile. "Actually, it helps tremendously."

Sobering, Luke apologized. "I'm sorry, but we'll need to ride hard until we get to the rendezvous point. But you can rest there. It's only another hour or two."

"I understand," Claire assured him.

"Ready then?"

Claire nodded, and Luke easily hoisted her up onto the saddle, then slipped in front of her. He cast over his shoulder, "Feel free to hold on or lean against me. If you get sleepy, tuck your hands beneath my gunbelt so you don't slip off."

As they rode, Claire commented, "I noticed the gun. You never carried one before. Can you shoot?"

Luke laughed. "Yes. But this was Gustaf's idea. I hope I don't have to use it." Silence prevailed until Luke remarked, "The Anderses are going to be worried about you."

"I imagine they'll figure out what happened."

"Somehow we'll have to let the others know you're all right." With this thought Luke grew pensive. The night also grew still, except for wild animal calls and Queenie's hooves and creaking saddle gear. The solitary Indian trail led deeper into the woods. As they clipped along, Luke was thankful for the moonlight so he could distinguish the ordinary shadows from any potential lurking captors. He dodged the branches that reached out to apprehend.

After considerable time had passed, Luke became more comfortable with the wooded surroundings. He mulled ideas over in his mind. With a pat, he checked his shirt pocket to see if Gustaf's letter of introduction was safe.

It would present him to the Sweeneys of Cincinnati, Gustaf's sister and brother-in-law. Gustaf had vouched that they would accommodate him. He could make the trip in two days if he rode hard and kept to the main roads. But with Claire and Davy, he might be recognized. They would need to travel cross-country as much as possible. It would be tedious.

Claire's sudden grip at his waist alerted him. Then he heard it, too, the approaching hoofbeats of several galloping horses. Instantly, Luke veered off the trail, and a branch knocked off his hat, which landed alongside the road.

But he spurred Queenie on through a tangle of tiny oak saplings and poplars while the sound of men on horses grew louder. After maneuvering Queenie behind a huge maple tree that hid them from view, they waited for the riders to pass. He patted his snorting beast's quivering neck, hoping to quiet her.

The sudden change in gait woke Davy, and he let out a shrill cry. Luke felt Claire shift, seeking to quiet the child. He scanned the area frantically, mentally planning their escape route should it be necessary.

"Whoa! Hold up!" Luke froze at the words, hoping Queenie and Davy would remain still. Scarcely breathing, Claire listened, also stiff and motionless.

"Let's make camp here." The menacing voice seeped of power and evil. "Billy, search around for a good spot. We'll let Sid and Red catch up with the loot."

Luke whispered, "They're stopping. We've got to get out of here."

Gently, he coaxed Queenie backwards, then reined east toward the wood's heart. Luke hoped the ground was grass covered, and he twinged at each snapping twig. Bushes swished as they inched away. They were about out of danger when Luke heard it, the dreaded discovery. "Look here! A good hat!"

"Let me see."

The hair on Luke's neck bristled, and his every impulse screamed to make a run for it, but listening to intellect, he continued at a cautious gait. The men were still too close and might hear them. And the woods were thick and dangerous. When a safe distance finally separated them from the band of robbers, he muttered aloud, "Thank You, Lord."

Soon they came onto the Indian trail again. "The road must curve," he whispered to Claire. "We're probably only a couple miles away from their campsite." Luke looked both directions, then warily moved onto the trail. He whispered, "Hold tight!" and spurred Queenie into a gallop.

After several miles, when it seemed that

they were not being followed, he eased the pace. "You all right, Claire?" he asked over his shoulder.

"Yes. Who were they?"

"Outlaws."

Claire was quiet, and Luke informed her, "We've lost some time. If you and Davy are up to it, we'll keep riding hard now. It can't be much further."

"Yes. Let's get out of here."

A myriad of brilliant stars canopied the moonlight riders. Luke gazed heavenward at God's handiwork and hoped he was in the Father's perfect will for his life. He frowned. What could he do about it now except concentrate on the task at hand? He scanned the trail ahead where the moonlight afforded vision, and he pricked his ears to listen for the approach of riders.

Even so, without warning, a haunting cry pierced the air, and terror shot through Luke's heart. Claire's small hands grasped his waist and clung. He whispered in a tremorous voice, "Just wolves, nothing to worry about." But his hand slipped downward to rest against the gun strapped to his hip. Eventually, her grip relaxed a bit until an owl's shrill hoot directly overhead startled them again.

Nearing one o'clock of the wee hours, they reached Sugar Creek. Luke reined Queenie to the water's edge and turned to Claire. "This is it."

"Where are we?" she asked.

"Sugar Creek, where we're to make our switch."

"But no one's here."

"Not yet," Luke said. "Let's look around." He pointed. "Over there's good cover."

On foot, they investigated the rocky shoreline area Luke had indicated. Deciding that it would serve as an adequate blind, they rested on a large boulder as Davy slept through the sounds of the shallow creek's rushing waters and night chorus of croaking frogs.

"You won't actually let them take Queenie, will you?" Claire's unexpected question startled Luke.

He squirmed uncomfortably. "No, it's not that kind of switch. Ssh! Listen! I hear riders! Stay put 'til we know who it is."

Two horsemen appeared in plain view on the other side of the stream, pausing at the road's end. They gazed across the water, talking between themselves.

"It must be them," Luke whispered.

Hardly a moment later, one called across, "Wheeler! You over there?"

"It's them, all right. But I don't recognize 'em. Wait here." Luke mounted Queenie, urging her slowly into the stream. When the two men saw him emerge from the brush, they, too, entered the shallow creek. Claire watched the riders meet halfway, where the moon cast an eerie silver glow across their partly discernible forms. She heard talking and even laughter as they all came towards her.

Luke motioned her to the craggy edge along the western bank. One of the strangers dismounted, then joined his partner to ride double. At the same time, Luke slid off Queenie. In a low voice meant for Claire's ears only, he said, "I think it's best if you go on with me for now. I'm sure these men are harmless, but I've never laid eyes on them before. Are you willing?"

She clung to his arm. "Oh, yes, Luke! I'd much rather go with you."

"That-a girl. Since you'll have your own mount to handle, why don't I take Davy with me?" Claire allowed Luke to disassemble the baby carrier and helped him into it.

Davy woke, overjoyed to be in the arms of his father. "There little one, how's that?" His son's reaction warmed Luke, and he gave Claire a cheery smile. "Now, let's get you mounted."

"What's his name?" Claire asked, sitting atop a black mare.

One of the strangers laughed. "Just like a woman. Wants to know the horse's name."

His partner grinned. "Sorry, we don't know, Ma'am."

"Well." Claire thought a moment. "I think I'll call him Moonlight."

"Her, Ma'am," the older man corrected.

Claire giggled. "Oh! *She'll* be Moonlight then."

"Why is that, Ma'am?" he asked.

"If it weren't for the moonlight, she'd be too black to see." All three men laughed at her reasoning.

Growing serious again, Luke thanked them. "I'm beholden to you for your kindness, the risk you're taking in helping an escaped convict."

"Ah, no," the younger one answered, "glad we could be of help." Luke eased Queenie next to their horse to stretch out his hand. Both men shook it.

The older one said, "A fine-looking boy you got there, Rev. Wheeler. Good luck to ya."

"Thanks. God go with you."

Luke's benefactors left them to head back across Sugar Creek, and he nudged Queenie into step beside Moonlight. As they also returned to the trail, he explained, "With them riding double like we were and then doubling back to Beaver Creek, anyone tracking us will follow their trail. When they discover we're not in Beaver Creek, we'll be almost to Cincinnati. Hopefully by the time the posse sees they've been duped, our trail will be too old to follow."

"I think it's a good plan."

"In a few minutes we'll come to Beaver Creek Road; only we'll head away from Beaver Creek, south toward Cincy."

Claire nodded.

"Now, we can take it easier. Let's ride for a couple hours, then find a place to camp and get some rest. Can you make it a few more hours?"

"Yes. I'm all fired up!"

Luke laughed. "So is Davy!" Then beneath his breath he murmured, "Poor child."

As promised, a few hours before daybreak Luke found a spot to camp. Set back from the trail, even at this dark hour he could tell it was a perfect spot. The tall grass was enough to hide them, and a brook rippled close by. The sound of water was what led Luke to discover it. There was evidence of previous campsites.

Tired as they were, Luke cared for the horses while Claire tended Davy. Soon camp was made, and two bedrolls were laid out just a few feet apart. An awkward moment occurred when both Luke and Claire realized the indiscreetness of the situation.

Luke cleared his throat. "Sure am glad for the extra bedroll those fellows had on Moonlight."

Claire turned slightly so the darkness would hide her burning cheeks. She chided herself for being so self-conscious after everything else that night.

However, Luke was having similar thoughts, and not for the first time. Every time her grip had tightened about his waist, he'd winced — knowing the impropriety of their wild ride. Would authorities think he had abducted her? Wasn't he responsible for her reputation now, as well as her and Davy's safety?

Suddenly weary, he said, "I'll sleep facing the road. Davy can bed with me. My son and I need to get reacquainted, and you need your rest." He politely turned his back on Claire then and allowed her to climb into her bedroll.

Snuggled up with Davy, his back still toward her, Luke murmured, "Claire?"

"Yes."

"Don't be afraid. We're perfectly safe here."

"I'm not." She sighed. "Too tired."

"Me, too. Come daybreak, we'll move on. This is a good place for the horses to graze and water." In the quiet Luke heard Claire's slumbering breathing. He smiled and kissed Davy's cheek.

CHAPTER 9

The sound of a woodpecker in a cotton-wood tree roused Luke to his first morning thoughts. Today he would hang! But he quickly shook it off as a blurry meadow setting focused. The wild ride through the woods wasn't just a dream then. As his head began to clear, he turned to corroborate his still foggy recollections. The gray bundle would be Claire. However, his movement was impeded by a small lump in his side. Whereupon he felt a little kick and rolled over to look full into his son's upturned face.

"Good morning, Davy," he whispered, cupping the baby's silken head within his palm. "Wide awake and not complaining. You're such a good boy; you deserve better. If your ma could only see you."

Davy cooed, blowing little bubbles from his parted lips. Luke lifted the baby to his shoulder as he raised himself into a sitting position. Eager now to examine their surroundings, he kicked off the scratchy woolen blanket.

Two revelations occurred simultaneously. First, this was a beautiful place; and second, it remained quite a contrast from the gallows prepared for his use this day, were it not for his escape.

All about him, two-foot-high cordgrass glistened wet with dew. Several yards beyond Claire, a brook gurgled. Birds dove from cottonwoods that lined its shore. Patches of bright golden asters dotted the meadow with yellow petals, welcoming in the new day. This magnificent display of nature cheered Luke after his weeks of dreary confinement.

Playfully he tickled Davy under the chin with his forefinger. "Let's clean up a bit." They stole past Claire and squatted by the creek's edge where Luke splashed his face. With a groan, he remembered his disheveled disguise. He took off his shirt and lay Davy on it, then scrubbed furiously, going so far as to dunk his head under the icy water. The vigorous head shaking that followed made Davy giggle and thrash his arms and legs wildly in the air. Shivering, Luke buttoned up his shirt again. Stubborn tree sap still adhered to his chin. Unconsciously, he scratched at it as he contemplated whether to build a fire.

"Luke!" A frightened cry broke the silence.

"Over here, Claire."

"Oh."

Instinctively, Luke turned toward the meadow bedroom. Claire sat with her golden-spun hair spilling all about her face, down her arms, shoulders, and back, her eyes still sleepy.

Only on Miriam had he ever beheld such a glorious sight as a woman's morning hair. Never before had he even considered Claire as a woman to be desired. The idea struck now that the two women were perfect contrasts, yet Claire was every bit as lovely as Miriam. He wondered when that had happened, having known Claire since she was a child. Her hair was as flaxen gold as Miriam's had been dark and shiny. Naturally, he compared the two. Claire was soft and tenderhearted; Miriam, vibrant and joyful. Miriam . . . was gone.

This abrupt realization brought Luke back to the present, where he was mortified at the realization that he was gaping shamefully. And upon seeing Claire's blush, he tore his eyes away, turning back to face the brook. Eventually he managed to put his straying thoughts in order.

A rustling sound alerted him that she was moving about. It sounded like she might be rummaging through the saddlebags. Why hadn't he thought of that? Suddenly curious, he wondered what supplies they did have.

From directly behind him Claire's voice, though soft and musical, startled him. "Things look different in the morning's light." His jump prompted her to giggle. "I'm sorry. I didn't mean to frighten you."

"Silly, isn't it?" he said shakily. "Just edgy, I guess." He glanced up and met her gaze as she settled beside him on a flat gray rock. With much relief, he noted her hair was once again braided and tucked away.

"Davy's last bottle," she offered. "Can I change and feed him for you?"

"Sure." Luke jumped to his feet and scooped the baby up, depositing him into Claire's lap. The child let out a cry when he saw his breakfast.

"Gotta check out supplies," he said and turned away, suddenly unnerved by the responsibilities that bore down upon him. Traveling with Claire unchaperoned could taint her reputation, and Davy was on his last meal. Then there was the danger of getting caught. "God help me," he whispered under his breath as he jerked open the flap on a leather saddlebag.

A glance skyward told Luke it was about six-thirty. Because of the remoteness of their campsite, they had not seen or heard any other riders. With that in mind, he decided to start a small fire and gathered the items needed for coffee and bacon.

By the time Luke had their scanty breakfast prepared, Davy was already fed and changed, and Claire groomed. When their meal was finished, Claire remarked, "You should try some bacon grease."

"Pardon?"

"For the tree sap."

"Oh." Luke rubbed his chin. "Think that would work?"

Wordlessly Claire plopped Davy on his lap and plucked a nearby trillium leaf, which she dipped into the fat. She tapped it with her finger to test its temperature, then smiled in satisfaction. "May I?" she asked.

"Be my guest," Luke stated.

She knelt down before him, her face within inches of his, and he closed his eyes. Carefully, she patted on the fat, then rubbed, scratched, and peeled at the sap.

"Ow!"

"Sorry."

After several minutes, she said, "There, go wash that off."

With a scowl he opened his eyes. The smirk on Claire's face irritated him. "I think you enjoy torturing me," he snapped. Maintaining an injured expression, he headed back to the creek, and when he returned, she had cleaned up the traces of their meager meal. "How's that?" he asked.

"Aside from the red raw blotches, it's a major improvement."

"Really?"

Claire giggled. "I'm sorry, Luke, but you looked so funny with your powdered hair and silly gray beard."

Luke grinned. "It did the trick, didn't it?" He strapped on his gunbelt. "Now we have to make plans. As long as there's no travelers, let's stick to the road. Odds are we'll come across a farm or cabin where we can get milk for Davy. I guess that's our next objective." He frowned. "Aside from dodging the law."

Back in Dayton, Sheriff Watson carried Luke's breakfast to his cell. As he twisted the key in the padlock, he frowned at the lump under the covers. "Rev. Wheeler, I got your breakfast here." No movement occurred. Sheriff Watson removed the key and pulled open the barred door. Inside, he started toward Luke's cot, suddenly suspicious. Standing over the lump momentarily, he jerked back the covers. With a curse he burst from the cell, slammed the plate he carried down on his desk, and stuck his head out the jailhouse door.

"Deputy!" he hollered at the top of his lungs. Grabbing his hat, he sprinted across the street. Within minutes he reached the small café where Deputy Galloway customarily dined each morning after his evening shift.

Heads turned toward the door when Sheriff Watson entered the café, breathless. Instantly, Galloway was on his feet. "What's wrong?"

Watson motioned his younger aide outside, then he wheeled and demanded, "What happened to Wheeler?"

"Wheeler? I don't know. What do you mean?"

"He's gone. His cot was stuffed with sheets, but the cell was empty."

Deputy Galloway squirmed. "I don't know. I'm sure he was there last night."

With another curse Sheriff Watson mumbled, "C'mon." They started back toward the jail. "We've got to get to the bottom of this. So start remembering!" Pale faced, Galloway struggled to keep up with the other lawman. A few strides later the sheriff added, "There'll be a posse to form."

A few hours placed many miles behind Claire and Luke. They topped the peak of a small knoll, and Luke halted Queenie. "Look!" He pointed down at a valley where the road meandered like a river through an open area spotted with clumps of trees and several cabins, corrals, and a barn. "Looks like Davy's lunch might be just ahead."

Claire nodded, her expression a mixture of relief and dread.

"We'll have to come up with a story." Luke had mulled this around in his head all morning, but he felt uncomfortable voicing it. He suggested, "We're a family on our way to Cincinnati. We're going to —"

"Luke," Claire interrupted, "I don't think they'll believe I'm Davy's ma."

He stared at her a moment, frowning, then the implications of Claire's remark struck him, and he despised himself for his obtuseness. "Oh. Of course I wasn't thinking."

Both were thoughtful a moment, then Luke began again. "How about . . . my wife died, you're her sister, and we're taking the baby to your family." He shook his head. "It's still not proper for us to be traveling together, but I guess there's no way around it."

"I think it'll work. It's closer to the truth, which will be better if questions are asked."

Without warning, Luke exploded. "I hate to lie, Claire."

"Maybe we won't have to."

Clenching his jaw in determination, he said, "Let's go."

They stopped at the first dwelling. "Wait here," Luke told Claire as he dismounted.

With Davy still harnessed to his chest, he started toward the small plain cabin. He knocked. After several minutes, an unkempt man with a surly expression opened the door. Rifle in arm, he scowled at Luke and the baby. "Yeah?"

"We're traveling and wondered if you could spare some milk for the baby?"

The man looked beyond Luke at Claire, his expression skeptical. "I'm feeling poorly and would rather you just moved on." He motioned toward the road with his blue linsey-sleeved arm. As he did, a suspender fell off his shoulder and hung in disarray against his untucked shirttail.

Luke hesitated, surmising that the man was nursing a hangover. When he was about to leave, the man stopped him.

"Wait. There's a cow out back. If you want to milk her, go ahead."

"Thank you." Luke reached out to shake

the man's hand, but he held it palm up.

"Ten cents."

Luke's eyes bulged. He had not expected the man to charge him, much less so extravagantly. His face grew hot with anger. Such options. Either he could take the man's offer or give him the verbal setting down he deserved, only to have to repeat this humiliating process all over again at the next cabin.

There was no choice. Reaching into his pants, he withdrew the coins and dropped them in the man's grimy paw. Then as he stepped down from the landing, the man called after him, "Stranger! I'll be a-watchin' you. Don't take anything that don't belong to ya, or ya'll be answerin' to this." He waved his rifle in the air.

"Don't worry, the milk's all I want," Luke snapped.

"Hmph!" The man closed the door and stationed himself by the window as Luke left.

After three of Davy's bottles were filled, Luke lost no time in removing himself and his charges from the man's property.

Meanwhile, Sheriff Watson, Deputy Galloway, and the rest of their posse slowed their mounts at Sugar Creek's edge.

"Hold up!" the sheriff hollered, removing his hat and mopping his forehead with his sleeve. "Dismount! Let's check these tracks out before we cross."

Deputy Galloway knelt by the roadside. "Looks like Wheeler went on across. The other tracks belong to more than one horse."

Watson nodded. "He must be heading to Beaver Creek like we suspected then. Let's go get 'em, men."

The rest of the day passed uneventfully for Luke and Claire until late afternoon when huge black clouds rolled in overhead. Casting an upward glance, Luke grew worried, knowing they would need to seek shelter before dark. This was yet another crimp in his plans, for they could not camp out in a storm. If it were just him . . . but it wasn't. With Claire and especially the baby, it was too risky.

Therefore it was with great relief that Luke noticed a column of smoke a few hours later. Paused at a crossroads, he watched it rise above a stand of trees at least a half mile away.

"Look, Claire! Let's check it out."

It turned out to be a secluded, homey-looking farm. Upon nearing, Luke saw a woman and child drawing water from a well

and heartened at the sight of them.

"Looks better than the last place we stopped," he said to Claire. "Shall we see if we can stay in their barn tonight?"

The wind whipped, and Claire glanced skyward. The storm promised to be a sure thing now. In addition to its threat, her legs and back ached from riding. Gladly she consented.

As they started forward, Luke cast an unnecessary warning over his shoulder. "Be careful what you say.

"Hello!" Luke called.

The woman looked toward them, setting down her wooden bucket. A few drops of water sloshed over the top, and she swiped at her forehead where perspiration gathered and unruly strands of hair lashed across her face. A gust of wind billowed her skirt, making her appear stouter than she was. She bent forward to send the boy scooting. "Quick! Go get your pa, Matthew."

Luke dismounted and took a few steps toward her. Her expression was wary so he introduced his family. "I'm L—" He paused, wondering if he should use his real name. "I'm Lyle Smith, Ma'am. This is my sister-in-law Chloe and my son, Davy." He cast Claire a guarded look.

The lady nodded. "I'm Elizabeth Jenkins.

My husband, John, is in the barn doin' chores."

Claire gave Luke an encouraging nod, and he continued, "We are traveling to Cincinnati. It's a long story, but we'd be obliged if you'd let us bed down in your barn tonight, with the storm coming in."

Before she could respond, the boy returned. "Pa's comin'," he panted.

She motioned for her approaching husband to hurry. "John!"

"Howdy," the farmer greeted Luke warmly.

"Lyle Smith." Luke held out his hand, then nodded at Claire. "Chloe and Davy."

"They're traveling and want to take shelter in the barn, John," the woman explained.

"Nonsense!" he said. "You'll stay at the house. Right, Elizabeth?"

"Sure." Elizabeth smiled. "You can have Matthew's bed."

"That's hospitable, Ma'am," Luke said. "Perhaps Chloe and Davy can accept your offer, but I best stay in the barn." At their perplexed expressions, he explained, "I don't think you understood. Chloe is my sister-in-law."

Elizabeth nodded. "Oh, yes, you did say that. You can stay in the barn then. Yes, that would be fine."

Luke pumped her hand up and down. "Much obliged, Mrs. Jenkins. I was worried for the baby."

"Why, of course you were." She turned to Claire. "Why don't you and Davy come with me while John shows Lyle where to stable the horses?"

"Matthew," the woman called over her shoulder, "can you fetch the water bucket? Then fill up another one for our guests?"

"Sure, Ma," the young boy answered.

"We best get those horses taken care of," John said, "before the storm hits."

Stretched out on sweet smelling hay, Luke lay warm. The barn he shared with the horses and other animals was dry and nearly draft free while outside the wind howled and rain pelted down upon the barn roof. Before he drifted off, he thanked God for providing for their needs. The Jenkinses were surely an answer to prayer. They had graciously offered shelter for as long as the storm prevailed with no questions. With Claire and Davy safe inside their house, Luke was able to get a good night's rest.

The storm turned into a full-fledged fury that blew throughout the night and the next day, finally moving on that following evening. To pass the rainy hours, Luke

helped John with his chores and some repairs the man had saved for such a time. Inside, Claire washed out Davy's diapers, hanging them on a makeshift line that stretched across the entire kitchen. She stewed over their slow drying while at her feet, Matthew played with Davy — until he left to plead with his mother for a baby brother.

As Luke worked over a broken harness, his spirits plummeted. He hated the delay the storm had caused even though he was thankful that, unquestionably now, their tracks were washed away. Out the open barn door, he could barely see the house through the downpour.

Wondering about Claire's activities, the idea struck that maybe he should leave Claire and Davy here and go on alone — but her face came to his mind, and with it he envisioned her uneasiness and reluctance to accept such a plan. No, that would never work.

When Luke entered the house at supper-time, the clothesline and its attachments had been cleared away. The meal was hot and filling and did not provide a time for private discussion with Claire. After the meal he pulled out Claire's chair and whispered, "We need to talk."

She nodded. "I'll help with the dishes first."

Luke followed John out to the porch with a cup of coffee. "Much obliged for all your help," John said after a few minutes.

"The least I could do. We appreciate your hospitality."

"The air smells good after a rain. But it looks like it'll be clear tomorrow."

Luke agreed. "We should move on. In fact, I need to talk with Chloe before I turn in. Thanks again." Luke left him to return to the house and find Claire. He wanted to tell her they would be leaving early the next morning.

In the sitting room, Elizabeth rocked with mending upon her lap and Matthew perched on the hearth, chipping away at a block of wood with a pocketknife, but Claire was nowhere to be seen. "Is Chloe around?" Luke inquired.

"She's in the bedroom feeding Davy." Elizabeth waved a threaded needle in the air, consent that he should enter.

The door to the adjoining bedroom was ajar, so Luke eased through the opening, careful to leave the door open. However, he stopped at the sound of Claire's voice.

She was poised on the edge of the bed with her back toward him, humming and talking intermittently while feeding Davy. The sweetness of the scene touched him, and he paused to watch, thinking about Miriam and wishing she had been able to hold their child, that he had been able to see her like that. When he came out of his reverie, he heard Claire speaking in liquidy-velvet tones to Davy.

"I love your father, you know. I always have, since I was twelve years old." Luke was shocked at her confession. But there was more. "Now I'm a grown woman and love him with a woman's heart. I'll never marry another." She stroked the baby's soft hair, and Luke, aghast, scarcely breathed. "Your pa's a decent man, strong of body and soul. He's the —"

Luke could not stand there any longer, letting her go on like that. He had to make her understand. "Claire!" At the sound of her name, Claire's face instantly paled, and her body stiffened. He slowly walked to face her, placing his hand upon her shoulder. "I'm so sorry, Claire." His eyes appealed. "But don't you see? You can't waste your life on me. I'm just an empty shell of a man."

"No!" She denied it.

"You don't understand." He persisted. "My love went with Miriam to her grave.

132

I've nothing left to give a woman." Her face began to color again, and his voice sounded quivery even in his own ears. "Even one as fine as you."

Unshed tears glistened upon her blue eyes, and his heart lurched denial. Ironically, for one who had just depicted himself as an empty shell of a man, terrible conflicting emotions surged through him.

"You're such a special girl," he began, then corrected himself, ". . . woman. On the other hand, I am a criminal, a wanted man, one without a future."

"But you're innocent," she blurted out with a great sob.

Luke slowly backed away, his voice filled with regret. "The law says I'm guilty. I should have stayed and hanged. You and Davy don't belong here like this. To make matters worse, it's dishonoring to your reputation."

A now trembling Claire jumped to her feet and pushed Luke hard, her blue eyes sparking. "Stop it, Luke! I'll not beg for your love," she snapped. "You! You intruded. Those words were never meant for your ears!"

He could only stare at her. In all the years he had known her, he had never seen such fury. He hardly knew how to respond.

"I–I'm sorry," he stammered. "I had no right. But please understand, Claire. I'll never love again."

"So I've already been told! And I shan't ask you to." Claire pointed toward the door. "Now, get out!" Davy let out a scream, and as she turned to the child where he lay on the bed, she shrieked, "See what you've done!"

Frustrated to the point of anger, Luke strode toward the door. Without turning he said, "We'll be leaving in the morning at sunup."

She glared at his back. "We'll be ready."

As Luke entered the sitting room, Elizabeth dipped her head low over her sewing, which gave Luke another setback, realizing she had overheard their argument. "Good night," he said, his voice cracking.

"Good night, Luke," she answered.

He flinched at the sound of his real name. "Your secret's safe with me," she added softly. "I hope you are innocent. I've grown to like you all."

Luke walked out without a word, stomping toward the barn.

CHAPTER 10

Luke felt more miserable by the mile. The image of Claire's red, swollen eyes — exceedingly angry as well as sleepless — were branded into his memory. She lagged several yards behind on Moonlight. The only words spoken that morning were those directed to the Jenkinses, expressing gratitude for their hospitality. Mrs. Jenkins's words also seared his conscience. "I hope you get your problems worked out. You seem to be such a nice couple. God go with ya."

Luke grimaced at the testimony he had left with her. The woman had no way of knowing that he was a Christian. But before he could commiserate long on it, another problem presented itself. A dusty cloud appeared on the horizon.

He pulled on the reins and turned to wait for Claire. In moments she caught up with him, chin tilted upwards, her face flushed and blue eyes snappish.

With one hand, Luke supported Davy's harnessed bottom where it rested close to his heart. With the other, he pointed ahead. "Looks like we got company. Better head for the trees." He tossed his blond head to signify which direction. In the quick glance he took at her, he noticed this new development had cooled the fire in her sapphires. Now they shone round and frightened. "Come on," he urged.

When Moonlight's rump disappeared into the stand of thick trees, Luke expelled a sigh. Things weren't going well. He paused to look over the area. With relief he spotted a worn down pathway straight ahead that veered off in the direction they were headed. Taking the lead, he cast over his shoulder. "Looks like we're in luck. We'll follow this trail for awhile."

Though the riding was easy, he wondered where this trail would lead. More outlaws? But the narrow path ran in the direction they were headed, so they continued on it in silence except for the sounds of forest animals and the crunching of twigs beneath hooves.

The slow gait allowed Luke to feed Davy without having to stop. Guiltily he wondered if Claire needed a rest. She was a grown woman. She could certainly ask if she had a need. But when the noonday sun radiated almost overhead, Luke knew a rest was long overdue and dreaded it. As his eyes searched for a suitable spot, his mind searched for fitting words of apology.

"This looks like a good place to lunch," Luke called back to Claire. Her weary expression distressed him, making him wish he had not been so stubborn. Quickly he dismounted, tethered Queenie, and went to Claire's assistance. "Let me get that."

Wordlessly she handed over the reins and stretched the kinks out of her booted legs. As she patted the wrinkles out of her skirt, her eyes downcast, she struggled between the desire to apologize and the urge to lash out in anger. Luke startled her with his touch. "Sorry," he apologized. Carefully, he spun her around. Words escaped him as he stood foolishly before her with his hand still upon her shoulder. He repeated, "I'm sorry, Claire."

His soft tone toppled her emotional teeter-totter. Her hands flew to her eyes, and her shoulders shook unmercifully. Naturally, he enfolded her in his arms like the many times he had comforted Miriam.

Claire cried all the more so Luke patted her back gently. He realized he did not know this woman. He had always thought she was so calm and controlled. Now the sobs kept coming until he hardly knew what to do next. Finally, she began to quiet. Should he speak again? Or would it make her cry all the more?

Luke cautiously released her. Tilting her chin upwards, he looked at her pathetic face. "I'm so sorry, Claire."

"No." She placed a hand upon his sleeve. "I'm the one who is sorry." She hiccuped while attempting a crooked smile.

"Why don't we sit down?" Luke pointed toward a grassy area, and she moved toward it while he removed Davy from the harness where he had been wedged between their embrace.

When the three had settled, Luke picked a few strands of grass, tossing them down again. He opened his mouth, but she spoke first.

"Please, can we just forget this?" She was staring down at her hands; Luke could feel her embarrassment.

"We've been friends a long time," Luke reflected aloud. "In fact, you're probably the best friend I have right now."

Her face jerked up, her gaze fastened on him.

"Of course we can," Luke said.

She hiccuped again and nodded.

The afternoon dragged long and hot even in the shade provided by the thick overgrowth of trees and brush along the unmarked trail they followed. Yet Luke found circumstances greatly improved over that morning's. Their backwoods route put them on the correct course toward Cincinnati. He had made peace with Claire, and Davy napped in his arms.

In Luke's complacent state of mind, he nearly nodded off. It was his sluggish reflexes that permitted trouble to befall them so easily. Claire's piercing scream was his first clue. He jerked awake. *Indians!* They blocked the trail. Panic engulfed him . . . How? . . . When?

A hideous scream rang out, and the braves moved simultaneously to encircle them. Instinctively, Luke reined close to Claire as the savages' painted horses closed in the ring. Luke's eyes darted, keeping all the braves under surveillance. Claire had gone mute; her eyes swallowed her pale face. Her hands clenched a white-knuckled grip upon Moonlight's reins.

Luke willed himself to be calm. He must appear brave. An Indian dressed in tan buckskins jumped off his mount. Instantly, two others followed suit. The redskin poked a long spear at Luke's face, and the other two waved knives and shouted taunts.

The spear was now tight against Luke's throat, pricking it. As he sat rigid, a few drops of blood trickled down his neck, and sweat ran freely down his stoic face. Davy let out a bawl, and Luke agonized. The Indian lowered his spear then and gently poked the child's stomach with it.

"No!" Luke yelled, turning the child aside.

The Indian muttered angry nonsense, but the ones encircling laughed uproariously. At the same time, a brave grabbed Claire's arm and tried to pull her to the ground. She screamed.

"Jesus!" Luke cried out loudly. "Lord God, deliver us!" The Indian's grip upon Claire disengaged as if she burned his hands. She trembled violently while Luke continued to pray with fury. "God have mercy! Protect us from our enemies!" Luke's voice boomed louder than any sermon he had ever preached. The leader grunted, and the Indians slowly retreated. "Thank You, Jesus! Lord, deliver us from the hands of evil!" The Indians continued to taunt the white couple though they mounted, widening the circle.

Luke eyed them warily. "Thank You, Jesus! Claire! Ride!" Luke whooped. They rode hard, side by side, through the gap, without a backward look.

"Thank You, Jesus." Claire joined Luke in prayer. Over and over, they murmured the words. When Luke saw an open meadow to the east, he hollered, "Come on, let's get back to the main road." Crossing it, they continued to veer east. Still they galloped until at last they spotted the more traveled Beaver Creek Road.

It was then Luke cast his first apprehensive look behind them. No Indians were in sight. "Easy, easy." He pulled back on the reins, and Claire followed suit. Still riding abreast, he panted, "Are you all right?"

"Yes!" The wind whipped Claire's fallen hair. Her eyes remained fearful. "But let's not stop!"

"I agree," Luke yelled.

They camped under the stars that night, about two miles from the lights of Beedles Station. So close to civilization, they felt safe. As they sat around the campfire, they talked in tones soft as the dandelion puffs in bloom.

Claire hugged her knees beneath her and posed a question, though she knew its answer. "I wonder what made the Indians turn away?"

Luke stretched his legs out long, his boots nearly touching the fire and remarked soberly, "They looked like they saw a ghost."

"God delivered us. It had to be!" Claire exclaimed. "I don't know how, but He did."

"Yes, it was God," Luke agreed. "Lately I can't seem to get any answers from Him. But today I have no doubt. He intervened miraculously."

"You must believe He still cares about you, has a plan for you."

Claire warmed at the way the firelight revealed, even enhanced, the dimples in Luke's thoughtful smile. "Yes. I feel very much in His hands tonight. Even though the future is unknown."

"Full of surprises," she said wistfully.

"Nothing will surprise me like you have."

"What do you mean?" Claire asked.

"It's your faith that spurred me on. But just when I come to depend on you, you get emotional and act like a woman."

"I am a woman."

"I know that now."

"Now?"

Luke rubbed his still raw chin, now stubbly as well. "Until a few days ago, I only saw you as a girl, Claire, a cousin." Gazing into her eyes, Luke remembered her words to Davy, *I always loved him.* If that were true, unknowingly he had hurt this girl . . . woman many times. He would have to be careful in the future. It still remained, he would never love again. Perhaps now was a good time to emphasize his feelings regarding their relationship. They were talking so freely.

"The truth, Claire, is through all this ordeal, you've held up better than most women, being the emotional creatures they are."

She lifted her eyebrows in teasing protest.

"I'm glad we're friends," he added.

She yawned and said sleepily, "Me, too, Luke."

"Time to join Davy?" Luke tilted his head towards the slumbering child.

"Yes," she murmured as she settled into her bedroll, which was warmed by the fire.

Bone tired, the travelers arrived at the outskirts of Cincinnati the afternoon of July 13. Heeding the instructions on the unfolded wad of paper extracted from Luke's pocket, they rode toward the heart of town. Main Street pointed them south toward the Ohio River, where they passed directly in front of the courthouse. Luke gave Claire a wary glance, then nodded at the deputy who lounged against its railing.

A market area lay just ahead. The aroma of tea, coffee, and leather mixed with a variety of vegetables, fruit, and cheeses beckoned. "Shall we stop to buy some milk for Davy?" Luke asked.

"Yes. I need to get the kinks out of my legs before we get to the Sweeneys."

Soon they were browsing through the port city's wares. Claire was intrigued with the women who passed, noting the styles in Cincinnati reflected the eastern cities. She welcomed the bustle of the streets after the lonely days on the trail. Luke, however, scanned the face of every person who passed. Worry rippled his forehead like a washboard.

Claire glanced sideways at him and admonished, "Relax. We made it!"

He gave a weak smile. "You're right." Then he pointed just ahead. "Hats, that's what I need." After trying on several, Luke purchased a tan beaver hat with a wide brim to replace the one he had lost on the trail. As he tugged at the brim, he asked Claire, "How do I look?"

Claire studied him wistfully from the hat down — blond bangs, clear blue eyes, crooked smile, and dimples. "Fine enough," she said, the color rising from her neck upward.

Luke threw back his head and laughed. "I feel like a whole man again." He pointed across the street. "How about a peach?" The fresh fruit, so much tastier than their dried rations, put them both in high spirits. Upon purchasing milk for Davy, they returned to their mounts, ready to complete the final leg of their journey.

They left the market area and rode past homes of various sizes, dodging children playing in the street. Luke kinked his neck to get a long look at a church they passed, wondering what denomination it was. Another market area, much larger than the first, appeared, and Luke told Claire, "We're getting close, according to Gustaf's map."

In minutes they approached Second Street, where they turned to Sycamore. On Sycamore, they headed toward the river again. Claire gasped. "Look!"

She pointed toward the Ohio River. Ships were bobbing in the waves like multicolored corks, sails topped the establishments, and as far as she could see there was blue water. "It's fantastic! I've never seen so much water. Are you sure it's not the ocean?"

Luke let out a whistle. "I'm impressed, too, but I know it's not the ocean. The moist air feels good, doesn't it?"

Claire nodded. "Mm-hm. Can we just stay

here a minute and take it in?"

"I feel that way, too. It's overwhelming."

After their eyes had scanned the horizon for several leisurely minutes, Luke asked, "Ready now?" Proceeding then, Luke overheard Claire's groan. He teased, "Better put on your brave face. We're nearly there." Then he nudged his mount forward.

They arrived at a tiny house, similar in many ways to the others that lined Sycamore Street, except this one was strikingly immaculate. Flowers nodded in the breeze, and a stone walkway snaked toward the porch. "This must be it, third house on the left. Let's go meet the Sweeneys."

At Luke's fervent knock, the door swung open, revealing a large-boned woman. She wore her blond hair, streaked with gray, pulled back tight then plaited and coiled about her head. Above rosy cheeks, inquisitive blue eyes thoroughly examined the threesome at her doorstep.

She saw a tall young man, fair and sporting a full mustache and stubbly beard. His face, though now contorted as if to form an opening remark, featured huge, fine dimples. Their points poked far above the unshaven portion of his lower face. His arms curved, cradling a baby.

The small woman with him was also fair,

with brilliant blue eyes and a slender nose protruding from a perfect oval face. Her once-white blouse and brown riding skirt were dusty and wrinkled, and the young lady looked capable of collapsing.

With concern Mrs. Sweeney asked, "Yes? May I help you?"

The towering one thrust a letter before her as he sought to explain. "My name is Luke Wheeler. This is Davy and Claire Larson. Claire boards with your brother, Gustaf Anders."

Helga Sweeney glanced at the letter of introduction, recognizing the familiar scrawl of her brother. "Won't you come in?" she offered in a friendly yet mildly cautious tone. "Please be seated." She mistook Claire's nervousness for fatigue and said, "You look about to faint. Allow me to offer some refreshment." Without waiting for their reply, she scurried off and returned with glasses of fresh water. Once their thirsts were quenched, Luke set about to tell Helga his story.

A full hour passed as he recounted his arrest and guilty verdict in spite of his innocence. During this time, Helga Sweeney's face revealed many different emotions. But when Luke told of the spectacular way her brother, Gustaf, had planned his escape, her eyes brightened with wonder. At times throughout the hour, Luke thought she was close to sending them on their way. But now the woman's countenance looked truly compassionate. When he had ended his account, she exclaimed with great emotion, "You poor creatures. Indeed! We shall be glad to help you out."

But even with the woman's assurance, Luke worried that her husband would appear at any moment and fling them out by their ears. He cast the thought off now as Helga patted Claire's hand and asked, "Do you mind if I read this letter from Gustaf now?"

"Forgive me for my rudeness," Luke replied, "by all means." He cast Claire a reassuring glance as they waited for Helga Sweeney to read her brother's letter of introduction.

"Why, you're a preacher yet!" she exclaimed. "Such repayment you have received for your kind deeds!"

By the time Ivan Sweeney arrived home from his day's work at his textile mill, Luke and Claire were feeling much better about the world. A bath and fresh set of clothes had been just the thing for Claire, and the promise of a safe haven made Luke a new man. Davy had been bathed and fed, and

Helga Sweeney — whose own children were grown — fussed over the child.

Thus her husband found them. "What's this, Helga," he boomed cheerfully. "We have company? And a wee one, too?"

"Yes, Ivan," Helga said excitedly. "These poor folks were sent here by my brother, Gustaf. They've had such a row of it." She began to describe the injustices as Luke stood and shook Ivan's hand, then politely interrupted to introduce themselves.

Ivan was also big-boned and tall. The Swede had friendly yet strong features despite his ruddy face and many freckles. Luke ascertained that the slightly graying, tow-haired gentleman was competent and well-respected among his peers. It was not long until he also discovered that both the Sweeneys were Christians. It was with gratitude that Luke accepted their pledge of assistance as well as their hospitality and friendship.

Over the evening meal, they discussed Luke's plight. Ivan, who proved to be a well of information, considered their options. "I can give you a job at my textile mill until something else comes up. My business takes me to all parts of the city, and I have connections in many areas. I assure you that your secret will be safe with us. Claire and

Davy can board here in our extra room. Luke, you can move into my small room at the mill on East Front Street."

Helga added to this. "It's on the docks but very close. Ivan walks it every day."

Luke replied, "I don't know how to thank you."

"Well, the night's still young, but I know you're tired. If you're agreeable, let's stable your horses and get you settled in at the warehouse."

Later, Luke stretched out on a long, soft bed. He smiled. It felt good to have a bed that fit. Of course, it had been made for the tall Swede. The room was used for times when business kept Ivan overnight. Ivan said it also provided a place for out-of-town guests.

In the lantern's light, Luke looked about him. This room was his for an indefinite amount of time. He smiled contentedly. How plush after his dreary, barren cell! There was a small fireplace with a stack of firewood to its left. By the glass window stood a stand with a flowered washbasin and glass lantern. A chair and small round table draped in a crisp cloth were in the corner by the door. Across the room was a desk equipped with stationery.

At this observation, Luke climbed out of the bed. He rummaged through the items in the desk. Now was as good a time as any to take care of something that had been plaguing him, to set Gustaf's mind at ease about Claire and Davy. He struggled with the wording. This missive must not be connected with him lest he give away his location. Finally, he wrote,

Gustaf, we received your three packages, two large and one small, in good condition. We will handle these gifts with care, in the same manner in which they were sent.

Your sister,
Helga

He would have Ivan post it in the morning.

With that accomplished, he snuffed the lantern and double-checked the door. It felt good to be on the other side of the lock. Content, he flung himself back into bed, yawned, and soon fell fast asleep.

The water slapped lazily against the craggy shore of the Ohio River where Ivan Sweeney's textile mill clung to the bank. Inside, Luke watched with fascination as the water-powered looms wove intricate designs of cotton and wool.

As Ivan showed Luke through his factory, they paused to watch a man carry a wooden block. Holding it by the rails, he dipped it in a tub of steaming red dye, then pressed it firmly onto stretched cloth. A Spanish woman gave it a firm tap with a wooden-handled mallet. When the block was lifted, the cloth was arrayed with tiny red flowers.

Ivan waved his arm, indicating the general area where they stood. "This is where I shall start you, Luke." As the woman prepared the cloth, Ivan explained, "This action is repeated until the design is on a whole length of fabric. Each color requires a separate block. The first color must dry before the second is applied." Ivan's face shone with pride. "It's time-consuming and labor intensive. A good place for you to develop some muscles." The Swede laughed good-naturedly at his own joke.

Luke looked down at his arms, still strong from years of farmwork when living at home. Though they had softened somewhat from his years of ministry, he knew his new friend was only teasing. "Is this the most physical work you have then?" Luke asked.

Ivan laughed. "No, not at all. But you must work your way up. Now, let's introduce you to your coworkers."

Luke soon discovered that the couple they had observed was married. He took an instant liking to the husband. Tony Diago, with his dark hair that curled from the steam of the dye vats, was dark-skinned as was his wife, Maria. Though not as tall as Luke, the young man looked strong as an ox.

Tony was a good instructor, and Luke quickly caught on to the routine. After several hours of laboring over muggy vats, Luke felt capable and began to converse while he worked. He was curious about the other couple.

"Were you born in America?" Luke asked Tony, while hoisting a wooden block and heading for the dye vat.

"Sí." When Tony looked up to answer, his face turned grave. "*!Tiñe cuidado,* señor! The vat is hot!"

With his attention focused on Tony, Luke had gotten carelessly close to the red tub of dye. As Tony feared — even with the warning — Luke's arm brushed against the great tub. With a howl, he dropped the block, which teetered precariously then started to slide into the vat. Instinctively, Luke reached for it then let out a yell, burning his hands as well.

Tony grabbed the red block from Luke, setting it on a nearby stand, while Maria attended the injured man. "Oh, poor Luke. It looks bad. I'll go after medicine." Maria ran from the room, her bright ruffled skirt swishing.

Meanwhile, Tony grabbed a chair. "Here, sit down, Señor. You look pale." Luke obliged Tony, who rolled up Luke's sleeve on the burned arm. At his touch, Luke gasped. "Oh, your arm's much better than your hands," Tony reassured him.

Maria returned with ointment for Luke's red, blistered hands and arm. "Better go see a *médico,* Luke," she advised. "It's near quitting time anyway. We'll tell the *jefe.*"

Luke prepared to leave then stopped. "Where is a doctor anyway?"

Tony grinned. "Come, Amigo, I'll show you."

"Does that hurt terribly?" Claire asked. Wrinkles lined her brow as she concentrated on the job of applying the doctor's ointment to Luke's severe burns.

"No, actually it's soothing." They sat alone at the Sweeneys' kitchen table. The others had retired for the evening.

"Seems I can't do anything right lately," Luke said.

"Nonsense, accidents can happen to anybody."

Luke looked relieved when the last dressing was finished.

"There," Claire said. "I'll be glad to attend to these until they are healed, Luke."

He nodded. "Thanks. The doctor said they should be good as new in a week." This reminded him. "The Sweeneys are so nice. Ivan is going to let me just tag after him for the next couple of days until my hands heal."

Claire's brows arched. "Going to learn the textile trade?"

"Never in my wildest dreams did I consider it . . . before yesterday. A person thinks he knows what he's going to do with his life then wakes up one day, and everything has changed."

"This is all temporary, you know," Claire reminded him.

"Maybe. We really don't know what the future holds, do we?"

"Well, I know what I'll be doing tomorrow," Claire said.

"You do? What is it then?"

"Helga is taking me to visit the orphanage."

"Really?" Luke exclaimed. "That's great!"

"Yes. Maybe I can get some ideas to take

back to Dayton."

Luke considered this then replied, "We need to make a plan, you know, to return you."

Claire grimaced. "Not yet, Luke. They'll be able to trace you."

"That's the problem. They'd question you for sure. I'll have to think some more about this. There has to be a way."

Claire grinned. "Anyway, you need me to dress your wounds."

Luke ignored her comment, pressing on with the issue. "Maybe we should send you to Beaver Creek for awhile to visit family. We'd have to find you a chaperone, of course. Then —"

"What about Davy?"

"I could hire a girl to take care of him while I work."

When Claire did not readily reply, Luke yawned. "It's getting late. I'd better go."

"Is your lodging nice?"

"Yes, very. Comfortable, too. And I'm tired."

Claire walked him to the door. "You've had a hard day. I hope you can sleep."

"I don't think I'll have a problem. Good night."

"Good night, Luke."

CHAPTER 11

A few days passed. One evening after supper, visitors called at the Sweeneys. Helga, who answered the door, recognized the callers. "Tony and Maria! How nice! Do come in," she invited.

As they entered, Maria took in the domestic scene. Luke and a blond woman occupied the settee. The pretty lady cradled a baby. With delight Maria squealed, "Luke! *!Trabieso chico!* You never mentioned you were married!"

Helga rushed forward. "Maria, this is Claire, and Luke's son, Davy."

Claire was afraid to glance Luke's way, knowing how he disliked deceit. She waited for him to correct Maria, but he did not.

"I'm pleased to meet you, Maria," Claire said. "Luke has told me all about you."

Maria giggled. "And this is *mi marido,* Tony."

Tony greeted Claire then said to Luke,

"We've missed you at work, Amigo. Well, we did get a glimpse of you with Mr. Sweeney."

Ivan interjected, "Luke is a friend of the family. Now that he's hurt, I can't allow him to stay with the women all day. I would get jealous. So I make him tag along with me."

Tony smiled. "Maria was worried when she saw your big bandage. She begged to come see how you fared." He motioned toward Claire and Davy. "Now that she learned you have *una familia,* perhaps she will not worry so."

Maria interrupted, "Sí, *marido,* and now I have made a new amiga."

Claire dressed Luke's burns again after the Diagos left. Usually these moments alone, within the intimate confines of the Sweeneys' kitchen, provided a relaxing end to the day. But tonight Luke seemed troubled. As soon as Claire finished, Luke withdrew his hands, folding them upon his lap.

"You look upset, Luke," Claire ventured.

"Just frustrated."

"What seems to be the problem?"

"I hated lying to the Diagos."

"It took me by surprise," Claire said. "However, if Maria learned that I was just your friend, they would ask questions. This way . . ." She shrugged with her hands.

"This way we weave a story of deceit. Now what will they think when you leave? That you deserted me? Or what if they discover I sleep at the mill?"

"Mm, I didn't think of that. If you're so upset, why didn't you tell them the truth?"

"I don't know. That's why I'm so frustrated. But it's not your fault." Luke digressed to mumbling, but Claire caught the remark: "Seems my whole life is turning into one deception after another."

Starting toward the door, he said, "Thanks, Claire, for dressing these." He held his hands in the air. His gloom saturated the room even after he left.

In the morning Luke walked out to the river as he did each day and gazed across the water glistening like a field of diamonds. Seagulls flapped and dove beneath the water's surface for their breakfast. Down the row of docks where vessels of all kinds were moored, fishermen readied their rigs for the day's catch. The shoreline was abuzz with early morning activity.

Luke wondered as he watched the men work. *How many are running from something, as I am? How many are caught up in deception, victims of foul injustices? How many —* A voice from behind startled him.

"Whot we got here? A runaway!"

Luke spun around, his body ready to spring into action. The face that leered into his belonged to Clancy. Luke gasped. He had never met the man but knew enough about him through Simon. "Sceered ya, did I? The last I heard there was a reward being offered for you."

The man eyed Luke from head to toe then chuckled. "It appears to be my lucky day." Then he sobered. "Are you dumb, Preacher?"

"What do you plan to do?" Luke's eyes narrowed.

"Well, I could turn you in and collect the reward, or you could save me the time with a gift to hold my tongue. My purse is gettin' pretty empty."

"Blackmail!"

"That's right. What do you think your life is worth? Three hundred?"

"I don't have that kind of money."

"Maybe not, but I s'pose with your neck on the block, you can come up with it." The man scratched his long beard. "Tell you whot. I'll give you two days. We'll meet here at the same place, same time as today. If you don't show, I'll turn you in." When Luke did not reply, the man turned to go. He stopped and threw a departing warning over his shoulder. "Don't forget now!"

As soon as the man was out of sight, Luke wheeled and ran inside to see if Ivan was at the mill yet. He knocked on his office door, which was closed.

"Come in."

Relieved, Luke pushed the door open.

One look at Luke's face brought Ivan out of his chair. "What's wrong, Luke?"

"Blackmail . . . Clancy."

"Whoa. Slow down. Who's Clancy?"

"Someone who recognized me from Dayton. He hangs around the docks."

"You sure?"

Luke nodded. "He threatened me with blackmail, three hundred dollars."

"What terms?"

"He said two days."

"Hm." Ivan looked troubled. "Better sit down, Luke."

Luke collapsed in a chair and pounded his fist against the armrest. "I'm done for."

"No. You have two days to find someplace else to go. We'll hide you someplace where he can't find you. Why don't you leave Davy and Claire with us until things cool down."

"I guess I have no other choice unless I want to give myself up. But where could I go?"

"You could disappear on the East Coast in a big city like Boston." Ivan frowned. "Or maybe you should go to the western wilderness. I doubt he'd follow you there. Wait a minute!" Ivan exclaimed. "I have just the thing! You said you wanted to work a job that took muscle?"

Luke grinned. "I have a feeling I'll regret asking, but what do you have in mind?"

"I'm putting some of my goods on a keelboat heading to New Orleans. You could go with it, become a keeler."

Luke leaned back in his chair, closing his eyes. Then he stared at the ceiling as if expecting his answer to appear there in bold letters. He let out a long, slow sigh. "I don't know, Ivan. It's dangerous, and it's harsh work." He held up his blistered hands. "Think my burned lily whites are up to it?"

"I think you're a strong man in body and spirit. You can do whatever you put your mind to. Think about it. It's only a suggestion. I'm sure there are many other options if you don't think it would suit."

"My strength is in the Lord, Ivan."

"All the better. The trip would take about three months. You'd be on the move. Surely folk would give up looking for you by then."

"Davy would be six months old," Luke murmured. "When will it be leaving?"

"Tomorrow morning," Ivan said apologetically.

"The timing couldn't be more perfect. Perhaps God is opening this door for me." Luke reflected, comparing his life of late to a river's current, swirling along with him trapped in it, unable to break free. What choice was there? "I'll do it," he said weakly. "I need to talk to Claire, make sure she'll take care of Davy. Then I'll be back and make plans."

"Good thinking. I'll start to make arrangements."

At his words, Luke strode away.

"Claire, will you get the door, please?" Helga called from the kitchen.

"Yes." Claire propped the straw broom she was using against the Sweeneys' stone fireplace. As she hastened toward the door, she wiped her hands on her apron. Who would be calling at this hour? "Luke!" she gasped at the one standing on her stoop. "What are you doing here in the middle of the morning?"

He smiled. "May I come in?"

"Of course." Claire stepped back to allow him to enter.

Luke decided that he would not let his own apprehensions show concerning his decision. The thought nagged at him that he was getting good at this deceitful stuff, but he quickly cast it aside.

"Something's come up. We need to talk."

Claire tensed. At once she assumed he had found a chaperone to escort her to Beaver Creek. With a frown she followed him to the settee.

"Are you terribly anxious to get home?" His blunt question, presented in such a pleading tone, puzzled Claire.

"No." Claire shook her braided head, "I'm not the anxious one. I never said I wanted to leave."

To her amazement, Luke did not argue. Rather, he seemed relieved. "Would you consider taking care of Davy for about three months? Here at the Sweeneys?"

Her blue eyes lit, and Luke saw the excitement in her face. "I'd love to! Why, if I stayed . . . I might even be able to help some at the orphanage." Luke nodded, and she continued foolishly, "Perhaps you could get a job there, too." Seeing his troubled expression, she quickly added, "That is, if the textile business doesn't suit."

Luke swallowed for courage. "Claire, I'll be leaving."

"What?" Her eyes snapped. "But why?"

"Do you remember Clancy from Dayton?" Claire nodded. "He's here, and he's found me."

"Oh, no!" she cried. "But that can't be!"

"It's true," Luke insisted. "He tried to blackmail me. Of course I don't want to go that route. So I have to leave right away."

"But where will you go?"

Luke grinned. "Keeling."

"I don't understand."

"Taking a flatboat downriver."

"I know what it is, but how . . . ?"

"Ivan has a load going to New Orleans. It's leaving tomorrow morning, and I'm going with it."

Claire frowned, her bottom lip stuck out, and the thought struck Luke that she looked cute that way. He flicked her chin with his finger. "It won't be so bad. It'll be an adventure."

"As if you haven't had enough excitement lately," she spouted. "And what about your hands? They aren't even healed."

"I'll be fine. Anyway, I don't have a choice."

"How long will you be gone?"

"Only three months. I'd be back sometime in October."

"Three months!" Claire gasped. "That's an eternity."

"That's why I need you to take care of Davy." Luke rubbed his forehead with a bandaged hand. "I really hate to ask you, but I don't know what else to do."

Claire's eyes instantly filled with pity. "Of course I'll help you. It's just . . ." Unshed tears stung. "I'll miss you."

Luke, so vulnerable himself, pulled her into his arms. He whispered, "We have been through a lot together these past few weeks, haven't we?" Claire released a tiny sob as she nodded. He continued to hold her tight for several moments. His heart melted. It was just as well that they put a little distance between them. He slowly released her. "I'll miss you, too."

The *Snappin' Turtle*'s patron, Henry Shreve, knew better than to argue with Ivan Sweeney. Ivan's strange request — that Luke be allowed to stow away on the *Snappin' Turtle* and learn the ropes of keeling — did rouse the seaman's curiosity, but things like that sometimes remained best unexplained. After all, Sweeney's textile business was vital to his own means of income, providing goods to transport on a regular basis. Then there was the fact that extra hands were always needed with casualties on the river being as high as they were. He just hoped this one could survive.

He lifted up the heavy canvas flap and peered down into the deckhouse. "You can come out now."

Luke blinked at the daylight, then crawled out from his hiding place and got his first good look at his twenty-odd crewmates. At first glance they appeared much like himself, being similarly clad. Ivan had provided Luke with the essentials — red flannel shirt, loose blue coat, brown linsey trousers, heavy boots, and beaver cap.

Strapped to Luke's waist was a wide leather belt that held a bowie knife. Unaccustomed as he was to carrying a weapon until the last few weeks, he also carried a pistol. He unconsciously rubbed his one-inch beard.

There was a major difference between him and the others. Their hands were calloused, and their muscles bulged like knots and knurls on a hickory log. Having spent several hours hidden in the cargo box, Luke heard the keelers before he saw them. They sang loudly as they ran the boards. Luke watched with fascination as the oarsmen worked, singing rhythmically. With a single sweeping glance he took in the entire crew of the *Snappin' Turtle.* His gaze paused at the stern, where the helmsman steered from atop a platform with a long oar pivoted to the boat.

Patron Shreve interrupted Luke's observations. "Sweeney said to take it easy on you until you were broke in. Says your hands are hurt." Luke nodded, relieved. "Well that is a shame, but we got work to do, and you'll have to do your share." Luke gulped. So that's how it was. "Understand?" The patron wore an expression that forbade Luke to question him, the owner and captain of the craft.

Luke nodded stiffly, thinking he understood perfectly — that he was in for a lot of trouble. Luke jumped when the patron bellowed, "Snake-eye!" A tall, tough-as-hardtack man of about thirty with long hair and one bad eye whirled and came to stand before his boss. "Over there." The patron motioned. Snake-eye stopped short of Luke, looking him over with his good eye. "This is Wheeler," Shreve said. "Show him the ropes on the broadhorn."

Snake-eye glanced at Luke's bandaged hands and snorted. "He looks soft."

"He is. And it's your duty to toughen him up, keep him alive. I'm putting you in charge of him." The order was just that, and Snake-eye compliantly though unwillingly motioned for Luke to follow. He set him to work at the broadhorn. As Luke pulled the heavy oar, black spittle flew past within inches of his arm, a reminder that his instructor was near, though silent and indifferent.

"Sawyer!" The warning rang out from the captain.

Snake-eye placed his thick, grimy hand on Luke's shoulder to wrench him from his post. Snake-eye then manned the broadhorn himself until the obstacle was clear. A loose tree had caught and now bobbed up and down as the current surged through it.

When the danger was past, he hollered, "All yours again, Whale," motioning with a muscle-laden arm.

"Wheeler," Luke corrected as he slipped into position. He wondered at his own courage.

The grimy hand touched his shoulder again while the one good eye challenged. "Like I said . . . Whale." He purposely accentuated the mispronunciation. "Sounds big, strong. You're under my care now, and I don't want a sissy following me around. Understand?"

Luke nodded, somehow heartened by the idea that the one-eyed keeler was taking him under wing. He only wished his hands didn't ache and thump so. And the rest of his body . . . sissy, Snake-eye had called him. The rest of his body would just have to get used to it.

■ ■ ■ ■

A westerly wind clipped the *Snappin' Turtle* along about five miles an hour downstream. By afternoon Luke was parched and bone bruised. His bloody hands still manned the oar; however, the wind now did most of the work. The blinding sun caused his head to throb along with his other body parts. Closing his eyes, he wet his lips with his tongue. He would have to grow his mustache longer to protect them.

"Take a break, Whale," Snake-eye ordered. Luke snapped open his eyes and nodded. As Snake-eye slid into position, Luke stood on the cleated footway that ran around the boat between the gunwales and the cabin. He stretched, then rubbed the welts on the back of his neck and wondered how the nasty insects had bitten him through his shirt.

"Hey, First-tripper!" Luke spun around and found himself facing a beefy, bald keeler with a bare, hairy chest and shoulders. A scar curved downward from his left eye to the corner of his brown, curly beard. He stood with arms folded above a firm stomach and his slanted eyes boring on Luke. "You hot, First-tripper? The flies biting you?"

"I'm fine," Luke retorted.

"I don't think so. Do you think so, Skinner?" Luke felt the presence of another keeler move in behind him. He cast Snake-eye a silent plea for help. But his bare-backed guardian shrugged his massive, sun-tanned shoulders noncommittally.

"I know what'll cool him off," Skinner said in a wheezy voice. He grabbed Luke by the back of his trousers and shirt, then tossed him to the floor like a sack of potatoes. Instantly, several pairs of hands flailed over him. Luke struggled, but to no avail as the keelers bound his hands and feet with a rope.

Luke's mind reeled. *They're going to throw me overboard. I'll drown.* He looked around frantically. *And no one is going to stop them!* But instead he was yanked by his hair into a sitting position. He wanted to lash out in anger, demanding they stop whatever hideous scheme they possessed, but he knew if he did, it would go worse with him. With this rough lot, he must act tough. He narrowed his eyes and clenched his jaw. His face shone red with anger. But what he saw next shot fear into his expression. The keelers roared with laughter.

Skinner was waving a sharp razor in front of Luke's face. "Want to know why they call me Skinner?" he wheezed. Again hilarity beset his mates.

Bluffing. He's got to be bluffing. "Not necessarily," Luke retorted with as much calm as he could muster. But the scarred one called Bones grabbed him by the hair again and stretched his neck until Luke thought he would lift off the ground.

Skinner warned, "Now don't move if the sight of blood makes you queasy, First-tripper." With that he began to shave Luke's head. Blond, damp curls fell upon his red shirt, onto his lap, and all about him. When his head was peeled slick and white as an apple, Skinner made to remove his mustache.

"No! Leave it!" Luke ordered.

"Oh?" Skinner liked the first-tripper's spunk and admired his courage. "Do you feel cool enough then?"

Streams of sweat coursed down Luke's bald head. He countered, "Like a snowy day."

Skinner wheezed, "You can keep the rest then, but your poor head's a-sweatin'. We got just the trick for that." Two men hoisted Luke off the floor, where he hung helplessly still bound, head down. Suspended by his legs, Luke thought he was going to throw up. His stomach lurched as the two slung him overboard, dunking and holding him underwater.

Luke gagged and came up gasping and choking each of the three times he was submerged. When he gave himself up for dead, he was suddenly hoisted back aboard and slapped down on the deck. His head hit the floorboards and again hands flailed over him until he was righted in a sitting position. Skinner blasted him several times across the back with his open hand until water spewed forth out of his mouth.

Snake-eye, who had been a bystander until now, commented, "Whale, that's what his name is." The others roared and remarked that his spitting did resemble a whale's waterspout and agreed that from then on "Whale" he would be.

"Whale, you're a good sport," Skinner said as he untied Luke's bindings. Then he gave him a final smack on the back, and Luke's bald head jerked. As his snickering tormenters returned to their posts, he sat there several minutes gasping for breath, glaring at Patron Shreve's back. The man had intentionally ignored the whole episode.

After Luke pulled himself to his feet, he half-stumbled his way over to Snake-eye, collapsing beside the man. "Thanks for your help," he sputtered. "I thought you were supposed to keep me alive."

"You ain't dead," Snake-eye snapped. "Couldn't be helped. Happens to all first-trippers sooner or later."

Luke glared at the man's one good eye. "Any more surprises I should be knowing about?"

Snake-eye smiled, the first human emotion Luke had seen on the man. "Perhaps. But I wouldn't want to spoil your fun, now would I?"

Luke sought to remain furious at the man, but for an unexplainable odd reason he could not. Instead, he found himself grinning back at his instructor.

"Keep your eye out for bears now," Snake-eye teased.

"Pardon?"

"Bear fat! It makes hair grow."

Luke groaned. Then Snake-eye surprised him even further. "Let's go to the cargo box and get some ointment for your hands." He pulled Luke to his feet and started toward the cargo box, pausing to call over his shoulder, "Better get your hat, or you'll get a sunburn." As Luke followed him to the cargo box, his spirits heartened. Somehow he felt like he'd risen a few notches in his crewmates' estimation.

The remainder of the day, Luke became

Snake-eye's shadow, willing to learn every task set before him. That evening the *Snappin' Turtle* moored at a wooded bank with a small grassy beach. "Get some rest, or you won't be any good tomorrow," Snake-eye warned Luke. "I'll bring you some grub later."

"Much obliged," Luke answered. As he lowered his body to a reclining position, supported by an elbow, he moaned. He leaned up against a sycamore tree and took inventory of his bodily parts. His hands had quit throbbing with Snake-eye's smelly ointment. He wondered what it was. His arms ached and burned, and his empty stomach growled. Removing his hat, he carefully felt his head with his blistered hands. He grinned. It felt soft as Davy's bottom. He closed his eyes and pictured his son, and Claire's face plainly popped into his mind's eye. His thoughts drifted then, and he fought sleep. He needed to get his bedroll out, to eat something, but he was just too weary.

CHAPTER 12

A week's ride downriver brought about many changes in Luke's physical appearance. His hands were rough and scabbed, his body was tanned and peeling, and his brown head a mass of peach fuzz. His body still protested, screamed at the long hours of punishment. But he had become accustomed to the routine, though never the men's vulgar language and crass jokes.

Many times he wondered if he would indeed survive this ordeal. At such times, indulging in self-pity, he imagined Davy going on in life without a father, envisioned Claire's tearful expression when she received the news that he had been killed. He shook off the thought. God was able.

Often if the others sang songs too coarse for Luke's liking, he would block out the lyrics by reciting Bible verses in his mind. Those in Philippians were precious to him, especially, "I can do all things through

Christ which strengtheneth me," and "But my God shall supply all your need according to his riches in glory by Christ Jesus." A favorite pastime with Skinner and Bones was tormenting Luke with horror stories of what lay ahead downriver. They warned him of the great falls of the Ohio that buried men and boats, sucking them alive into Hades, and spun tales about the killer pirates at Cave-in-Rock. Sea monsters, alligators, and any other leviathan real or imagined in the "Mrs. Sippi" were depicted in gory detail to the first-tripper.

A comforting factor was the alliance formed between Luke and Snake-eye. The man had taken him under wing, taking to heart Patron Shreve's order. On one particular evening, imbibed with liquor Snake-eye grew more talkative than usual. He seemed determined to know what Luke was about. "Why were you holed up in the cargo box when we left Cincinnati?" When Luke did not immediately reply, Snake-eye posed answers. "You burn somebody's house down?"

Luke laughed. He gave his hands a wave. "No, I burned these in a dye vat at a textile mill."

Snake-eye wrinkled his nose. "Sweeney's mill?" Luke nodded. "You running from a lovesick woman?" Luke stifled another chuckle, knowing Snake-eye would not be laughed at a second time and wondered what the man would come up with next. Snake-eye ventured again, "You're too soft for murder. How about blackmail?"

Luke choked. "How'd you guess?"

"Naw. What'd you do anyway?"

Without knowing why, Luke trusted the man. He found himself quietly pouring out his story, and Snake-eye did not once interrupt throughout the whole.

"Unbelievable," he exclaimed when Luke was finally silent. Luke thought he referred to his story; however, the man's exclamation surprised him. "I'm hooked up with a preacher."

Luke grinned. He had a hunch Snake-eye's own past was on the notorious side. "I'd be glad to hear your story sometime. Preachers are good at listening."

"Ssh! Get yourself in more trouble than I could handle if the others catch wind of this — that you're a preacher. Understand?" Luke nodded. Snake-eye continued, "That Clancy you talked about. I know of him."

"You do?" Luke leaned forward with anticipation.

"Yep. I also know something you'd find interesting. Clancy must consider blackmailing his livelihood. He blackmailed Aaron Gates and his son. He saw Aaron murder somebody."

"You know this?"

"Heard it in a pub in Cincinnati, before we headed out. He was bragging about it. That's how he got his fishing sloop, blackmail."

"You don't say? Why, that's helpful, Snake-eye. Say, do you know where I could send a telegram?"

"New Orleans."

Snake-eye's drunken smile made Luke leery, wondering what hideous thoughts were rolling around in the man's mind, but he answered, "Thanks for the information. I owe you."

Shawneetown, a mingling of Indians and whites, river rats of all sorts, was a last link to civilization. Following it came Cave-in-Rock's killer pirates and the Mississippi itself. Remorsefully, Luke watched the town disappear until it remained a mere speck which then vanished behind a curve in the river. Four more hours and they'd pass the dreaded pirate rock near Hurricane Island.

The wind whipped up, and all hands were called upon to keep the craft in the deeper water away from the rocky shoreline. Fighting against weather and current, they had to pick and shovel their way along. The four hours turned into six, making Luke's anticipation soar even higher until the feared warning rang out.

"There 'tis!" Bones exclaimed. "Hurricane Island!"

Patron Shreve shouted, "Gunmen, at your posts! Oarsmen, pull! Under no circumstances go near the shore nor stop 'til I give the order." The patron was pleased that things had gone as planned and they would not be passing the Rock at dark. Daylight hours provided ample time to sail well beyond the pirates' den before they camped for the night.

"Whale! Can you shoot?" Luke acknowledged that he could, and Snake-eye ordered, "Then get your pistol out and cover me while I man the oar."

Luke drew his pistol and checked to see that it was loaded. He had hoped that Cave-in-Rock was just a story Bones and Skinner fabricated to frighten him, but at the patron's reaction, he knew it was real enough. A sick feeling rose from the pit of his stomach.

"That's the Cash River," Snake-eye explained with a nod of his head. "Won't be long now."

The island was in sight. Smoke rose from the shore. As they sailed closer, Luke made out figures around the fire. Why, they did not look like pirates at all! They motioned toward the *Snappin' Turtle,* waving them ashore. "Stranded . . . ," he heard them yell. Luke looked at Snake-eye.

He shook his head. "A trick."

When the men on shore saw that the boat was not going to stop and that the *Snappin' Turtle*'s cannon was pointed in their direction, they ran for cover. However, before they were even out of sight, gunfire sounded, and the water splashed mightily beside Snake-eye. Luke wheeled, searching for the source. "On top!" Snake-eye cried out.

Luke looked up at the high cliff. Could gunfire be coming from there? He saw no one. Then another roar exploded, followed by a scream. Skinner fell to the deck. What Luke saw was ghastly. He stood stupefied, staring. Another blast jerked the boat, throwing Luke off balance. He fell to the deck, his gun misfiring into the air.

"Put down the pistol," Snake-eye ordered. "They're too far away now. Let the gunners take care of it."

"That was our gun?"

Snake-eye nodded as another blast from the *Snappin' Turtle*'s cannon hurled a ball of iron through the air. Luke watched Hurricane Island. Several blazes ignited, but all else was still. "Where'd they go?"

"Crawled back under the rocks they came out of," Snake-eye snarled. "That'll be the end of it for now." He looked sadly toward the bloody pool where Skinner lay sprawled. " 'Til we're going against the stream. We can't sail past then, we crawl by. We'll be lucky if we don't all end up like poor Skinner there." Snake-eye's words sobered Luke since the man had never stretched the truth.

Bones placed a canvas over his friend's body and then returned to his post, shoulders slumped. Another hour passed before the patron addressed his crew. At that time he congratulated them on their performance, pleased that the *Snappin' Turtle* had not been damaged, and expressed his condolences for losing a good keeler. Skinner was buried that night at camp. Luke felt sorrow for their loss, even if it was the one who had made him the brunt of his cruel joke. This crew was a tough lot, but they stuck together.

The *Snappin' Turtle* reached the port city of New Orleans in record time, four weeks. Patron Shreve gave the keelers shore leave while he bargained for their return cargo.

Luke shouldered his way through the busy streets of New Orleans, crowded with French Canadians, rivermen, traders, Indians, merchants, and buyers. The shop signs were printed in French, so he window-shopped. He needed to find a place to send a telegram.

"Bonjour, monsieur," a young boy greeted Luke.

"Hello." He smiled in passing.

Turning his attention back to the row of narrow French shops, Luke noticed a window display of maps. He drew close to peer inside. He was in luck! The shop seemed to be a hub for activities such as posting and receiving mail and assessing metals. There was a telegraph machine! Heartened, Luke entered and approached the counter where an elderly bald man stood stooped. Luke cleared his throat. "I'd like to send a telegram, please."

The man shook his head in perplexity, his wire-rimmed glasses slipping down his nose.

Luke repeated himself slowly.

"Oui, monsieur . . . telegram." The man understood and handed Luke a paper and pen. Luke wrote his message.

Dayton, Ohio. Simon Appleby. Clancy witnessed murder. Blackmailed Aaron

Gates and Ruben Gates.

"Non, monsieur. L'anglais est très difficile."
The old timer waved his arms in the air to
portray a problem.

*Why don't they hire someone who speaks
English?* Luke wondered. He rubbed his
chin, watching the tiny man who had now
turned his back on him. At the sound of
Luke's coins spilling out on the counter,
however, the man turned and nodded.
"Merci."

From beneath the counter, he extracted a
chart with the letters printed. Then the man
began the tedious job of picking out the
foreign words. Luke waited impatiently until
the entire message was sent.

At the last tap, Luke announced loudly,
"Thank you very much."

"Vous êtes bien aimable," the clerk replied.

With this task behind him, Luke departed
to search for Snake-eye. As he made his way
through the bazaar of festive carts and
stands, a dark-skinned woman with a daz-
zling smile called out to him. *"Marin! Venez
ici!"*

Luke shrugged his shoulders. "Sorry."

Quickly catching on, she tried again.
"Sailor! Come here!"

Her fluency of English surprised Luke,

and he hesitated a moment too long, allowing her to lean from her stall to bait him.
"Come see my wares." She fingered beautiful materials and silken scarves.

Luke blushed.

"A beautiful gift for a lady," she coaxed
with painted red lips that were much too
full. Her eyes were round and flirting. *"Oui?"*

"Go on," a voice beckoned from behind,
and Luke turned to see Snake-eye grinning
at him. "Good price," he urged.

The two men moved closer. Snake-eye
leaned on the stall as Luke self-consciously
fingered the scarves the woman held out.

"What color your lady's hair?" she asked.

"Blond," he answered weakly.

"Red one, perhaps?" she offered.

Luke smiled back. "But what will she do
with it? I've never seen her wear a scarf
before."

"I will teach you. Come." She winked at
Luke; then before Snake-eye could raise an
objection, she slipped the scarf around his
waist. To Luke she invited, "Now we practice."

Luke laughed loudly, enjoying Snake-eye's
discomfort. "It may take much practice," he
said.

She shrugged. "No problem."

■ ■ ■ ■

Everything was more terrifying, more strenuous, or more beautiful going fornenst stream — upstream — since they traveled at a mere snail's pace. Other river traffic consisted of Creoles, French Canadians, Kentuckians, tough, hard men from all parts of the world looking for adventure.

Luke's bare back, now toned with sleek muscles and tanned from August's toasty sun, rippled under his exertion. He easily thrust a twenty-foot pole with an iron point at one end and a knob at the other. The pole was like a third arm to Luke after six weeks on the river.

He worked together with the crew to the rhythm of the patron's chants, "Toss poles!" Spiked ends flew into the water. "Set poles!" Luke grunted as he set his pole into the riverbed. "Down on her!" Luke placed the knob against his shoulder and pushed with all his might.

With the keelers' combined efforts, they overcame the current and slowly moved upstream. "Lift poles!" With a grunt, Luke yanked his pole from the water and dragged it back to his position on the runway. Each time this process was completed, they managed to push the craft farther upstream.

Sweat poured off Luke's now fully bearded face and streamed down his strong back and muscular legs. His scarred, calloused hands were able to give the patron a good day's work. And a good day's work was keeping the craft moving at about a mile an hour.

"Gators!" Snake-eye drew Luke's attention across the river. Luke scanned the shoreline, locating the long, scaly reptiles that intrigued him so. Several lounged on the beach, some on rocks, lifeless. Others slithered into the river. Swimming eyes bulged above the surface of the water, distinguishing the alligators from floating logs.

Occasionally, a leathery tail slapped a rock, propelling a hungry alligator into the river. Nearby, churning water gave evidence of an underwater fight, wherein some unknown creature was becoming the reptile's meal. Luke watched in awe as the giant jaws gaped open and snapped shut, revealing for an instant the huge reptilian teeth.

This was just one of Luke's many unforgettable experiences. The crew, though unruly and crass, would also be forever etched in his memory and some in his heart. Daily he sought opportunities to witness to Snake-eye. However, the keeler would not allow such talk, making Luke wonder what sordid things lurked in the man's past.

One evening in early September, a storm arose. Some men always bunked aboard the craft while others camped ashore. This particular night Luke was in the cargo house on an undersized bunk being tossed from starboard to port side, it seemed. The wind howled, and waves splashed against the keelboat. Lightning ripped through the night, and the thunderclaps kept Luke wide-eyed. He prayed and thanked God that his journey was more than half over, for he had been pushing a keel now for eight weeks.

Luke thought of Davy as he did whenever he prayed, and he brought his son before the throne, as well as Claire. With each passing day, his desire to see her again increased. Her words splashed into his memory like a well-loved poem tucked away in the heart, "I love your father, you know. I always have. I'll never marry another."

A picture that replayed itself often was Claire in that meadow bedroom, her golden hair spilling all about her face, down her arms, shoulders, and back, her eyes still sleepy. He envisioned her cradling Davy, singing lullabies, smiling and looking up at him with her bright blue eyes. He remembered her touch when she had dressed his wounds, soft and tender; her embrace the day he left her, warm and alive.

Luke prayed for these memories to go away, but instead they became vivid and more enticing. His heart ached with loneliness for this woman. At the same time, calling up Miriam's likeness grew more difficult. Even his dreams of her were fading. With guilty pangs he grieved anew. How could he do this to Miriam? Why was God allowing this?

What would happen when he returned to Cincinnati? He was a fugitive. So maybe he did have emotions for Claire, deep-seated ones of love, loneliness, and fear, but the rest remained the same. He was a man without a future. If he sent Claire home, it would hurt her. Would it hurt her more if he loved her, married her?

The cargo room lit as lightning streaked across the Mississippi River's night sky, then fell dark again. Thunder cracked. Luke pulled his woolen blanket over his head.

At times when the river swelled too deep to touch bottom, the *Snappin' Turtle*'s crew cordelled their way upstream. This meant that some of the men swam ashore and towed the boat by means of long cordelles, or ropes. Put ashore this particular day,

Luke and Snake-eye worked to forge a path along the water's edge for those pulling the cordelles. Blood trickled down Luke's face where branches scratched him. Stickers and burrs clung to his beard from the heavy thickets. Wading through a quagmire, Luke poked at the swampy muck with his forked stick, slinging snakes into the river. Just ahead rose a rocky cliff, and they paused to look for the best place to climb.

The other crew members were a quarter of a mile behind them, so they leaned against the stone outcropping to rest. This gave Snake-eye a chance to question Luke about a concern he had been mulling over for the last mile. "It's a miracle we got by without any killings at Cave-in-Rock," he said, referring to their second encounter with the pirates on their return trip. Luke agreed, and Snake-eye asked, "You think your prayers really worked?"

"It's not a matter of my prayers working or not. God hears all prayers. He is in control of the universe."

"If that's true, then why did He let so many bad things happen to you — being a preacher and all?"

"I don't know. But I still trust Him because I know He loves me. Sometimes things happen just because of natural causes, or somebody else's sin. A man murders someone, it's his sin that causes the pain, not God."

"But why doesn't God stop it?"

"Because everyone makes their own choice about God and sin. If He stopped folks, then we'd all be just puppets."

"Humph!" Snake-eye grunted.

"But I believe if we trust Him, He will work things out for our good."

"You think that will happen to you? You sure you won't hang someday?"

Snake-eye's question was one Luke had considered many times over the last several months. "If I do, it will be all right. You see, then I'd be with the Lord in heaven."

Snake-eye remained silent. Luke spoke quietly, "You ready to meet the Lord, Snake-eye?"

"You know I ain't!" he snapped.

"Doesn't matter what you've done with your past, it's all forgivable. If you believe that Jesus is the son of God and died for your sins, repent and trust Him with your life. He'll forgive you, wipe your slate clean, and prepare a place in heaven for you."

"What's repent?"

"It means to change your sinful ways."

"Well, Whale, I'll tell you what. I'll chew on that awhile."

"Fair enough," Luke said.

They rose to begin their ascent when simultaneously they heard a deafening roar and a hideous human scream from somewhere behind them. Immediately they turned back to help their crewmates. As they scrambled toward the sounds of danger, their feet kicked up the swampy water, soaking them to their chests. Luke drew out his pistol, and Snake-eye had his knife ready. The horrendous sounds of a crazed beast's growls and a man's cries crescendoed, and horror flowed through their veins. Then a loud shot rang out, followed by two more, and the hideous growls ceased.

When they reached the rest of the crew, Luke was sickened at the sight. A bear and man lay dead in a heap, the man mangled almost beyond recognition. The crew stood stunned by the ferociousness and velocity of the killer. Snake-eye's gaze met Luke's. Without a word, each knew the other's thoughts; death is unpredictable. And now there was a grave to dig.

CHAPTER 13

On an unseasonably cold night in early October, the *Snappin' Turtle* docked in Cincinnati's port at dusk. Luke fell into line with all his mates to file past Patron Shreve and receive his pay of forty-five dollars for three months' back-breaking work. He pulled his beaver cap down tight against his ears to keep out the wet chilly wind as he shifted from foot to foot. Reluctant to say good-bye to the crew and apprehensive about seeing Claire again, Luke mulled things over silently.

Snake-eye cut into line ahead of him, and Luke squeezed the man's shoulder. "I'm going to miss you. You were a good instructor, a good mate."

"I'll miss you, too, Whale."

He held out his hand, but Luke unashamedly embraced the man. His voice was thick with emotion. "I couldn't have made it without you."

"Nor I you. After all, you showed me your God."

Luke fumbled with his bandanna, which encased his few belongings, and withdrew something dark. "This is for you, Snake-eye. Something I picked up at Louisville."

"For me?" Snake-eye's one good eye lit with pleasure. "Well I'll be, Whale. This is just perfect. I'll be the meanest-looking —" He saw Luke's frown and changed his thought midsentence. ". . . God-fearing keeler around." He slipped on the black eye patch.

"But I don't have anything for you. Maybe I can buy you an ale at the local pub?"

"Sorry, but I have a family waiting. Anyway, I don't drink."

Snake-eye grinned. "I remember. Old habits are hard to break."

"I have confidence that you will do so," Luke said.

After Snake-eye and Luke received their pay, they parted ways just outside of Sweeney's textile mill. It was closed up for the evening, but Luke knew where an extra key was hidden.

Claire answered the door and waited for the stranger to speak. The face beneath the beard seemed familiar. "Luke! I can't believe it's really you. Thank God you're back safe."

"Don't cry now. It's so good to see you, Claire. I've missed you."

"Oh, I've missed you terribly," she blubbered. "This is so wonderful. Come in!"

A six-month-old child rolling on the floor paused to see who had entered the room, his blond curly head tilted toward Luke. Luke rushed toward him, astonished at his son's growth, even though he had known it would be that way. The baby crawled as fast as his four limbs would carry him in the opposite direction; however, Luke scooped him up into his arms. Much alarmed, Davy screamed hysterically, flailing his dimpled arms and kicking his chubby legs.

Luke bounced, cajoled, and murmured to the child, but to no avail. "Davy, Davy. Come now, it's just your pa." Seeing that the child was not going to settle down, he finally relinquished him into Claire's outstretched arms. He clung tight to her neck and gradually diminished his crying while stealing glances at the stranger.

"Da-da-da!" Davy blurted out angrily.

Luke's face shone with surprise. "He talks!"

"I don't think he knows what he's saying." Disappointment laced her words.

"Luke, I'm sorry he doesn't remember."

Luke threw up his hands to stop her apology. "No, it's all right. Three months is a long time — half his lifetime, in fact."

"I'm sure he'll make up to you fast, probably by the end of the evening."

"Where is everybody?"

"They are visiting their daughter in the country. Ivan took the afternoon off. They should be home by tomorrow noon."

"That explains why I didn't see him at the mill. He'll be surprised when he hears we're back. The trip went better than usual, and we made good time."

"Why don't we go to the kitchen," Claire suggested, "and I'll heat up some supper for you while you tell me all about it." She set out coffee, cheese, and bread for Luke to nibble on while she heated up leftover stew, stirring as she listened.

"Oh, this is good," Luke said. "Half the time I honestly didn't think I'd make it back. Mm. Such comfort."

Claire smiled. "Was it really that bad?"

"Worse. You can't imagine. The first day aboard they hog-tied me, shaved my head, and dunked me overboard."

"They what?" Claire stared at his long, full beard in wonder.

"It's true. Of course it's grown back by

now." He felt her eyes on his face. "And, well this" — Luke rubbed his beard — "makes a good disguise." Claire laughed, and Luke liked the way it sounded — like bells.

She tested the temperature of the stew with the tip of her finger and licked it clean. "What else?"

"Well, there were alligators. Scaly, about seven feet long, heads about half as long as their bodies. Their teeth are enormous and their strong tails deadly. They crawl and swim along the banks of the southern Mississippi."

"Ugh! Are they dangerous?"

"If you get too close. Then there were snakes, yellow jackets, and chiggers."

"Chiggers?"

Luke nodded as Claire handed him a bowl of steaming stew. "Mm. Thank you." He took a huge bite, then talked between bites. "Part of the crew camped out on the shore, and part stayed on the *Snappin' Turtle.* These little mites are so tiny you can't see them, but you could sure feel them crawling under your skin."

"What did you do?"

"Rubbed them with ale."

"That relieved it?"

"Yep. Killed them."

"What about the crew? They sound mean."

"Rough characters. But after I got used to them, I could abide them. Even got to like a few. And made one real good friend, Snake-eye." Claire saw the admiration in his eyes. "Three men died on the journey. One drowned during a storm, one was killed by a bear, and one killed by river pirates."

"How awful!" Claire clapped her hand across her mouth. "I knew it must be dangerous. I'm just so glad you're here safe."

Luke knew someday he would share more of his adventures with Claire, but tonight he did not want to upset her further. "Sit here beside me, Claire." Slowly she pulled up a chair. "I thought about you a lot. I really missed you and Davy. You both mean a lot to me."

Claire wanted this moment to last forever, and she longed to reach across the table and touch his hand as she had the many times she had dressed his burns. However, his comment reminded her that Davy was out of her sight.

She rose from her chair. "Davy's too quiet." Luke pushed his plate away and followed her back into the sitting room to look for his son.

Davy had wadded a torn piece of Ivan's newspaper and was chewing on it. As Claire pried it from his chubby little fingers, he protested loudly. Luke suggested, "Maybe this will cheer him." He pulled a leather string of brightly colored beads from inside his vest pocket. The child's eyes lit with pleasure. "Come to Papa." Luke dangled the beads, enticing the child to venture closer. Soon he had Davy on his lap. He turned to Claire. "He's gotten heavy."

"Sixteen pounds now," she said with pride.

"Da-da-da," Davy babbled, clapping his hands. Even though the words were indiscriminate, Claire's eyes teared with joy.

They sat together on the settee, and after awhile Luke remembered. "Oh. I have something for you, too." He pulled out a tiny parcel and handed it to Claire.

With delicate fingering, she removed the wrappings. "Oh, it's beautiful." She examined the long red silk, letting it flow through her hands.

"May I show you how the women in New Orleans wear them?"

"You bought it in New Orleans? How exciting."

Luke grinned wide, then set Davy on the floor with his beads. He felt like a child with two new toys, not knowing which to play with, wanting to hold Davy, yet wanting to be close to Claire. He stood and motioned for her to join him. "May I?"

She handed him the scarlet scarf and carefully he encircled her waist with it. His grip on both ends of the scarf, he tugged until she stepped toward him. His tanned face was within inches of hers. Claire's blue eyes transfixed him. Slowly Luke leaned forward and placed a soft kiss on her unsuspecting lips.

When he pulled away, he said breathlessly, "I didn't plan that."

Claire blushed, still in the confines of his grasp upon both ends of the scarf. His tender gaze almost did her in. He fumbled then at her waist to tie the scarf. "Hold still now," he teased. Though his hands trembled, he felt such contentment, such joy at her closeness.

When he released her, she was much surprised to see a knot that resembled a rosebud. "It's lovely. How did you learn to do that?" Her eyes and tone were mildly accusing.

He rolled his eyes. "Don't ask. Perhaps I'll tell you someday."

"Another one of your adventures?" she teased.

"Exactly."

Wanting to change the subject, he knelt beside Davy, tickling him under the chin. The child giggled. "It's about your bedtime I imagine. I'm looking forward to a good night's rest myself, one without worry. Good night, Son." He took Davy into his arms and kissed him. Davy pulled away from his face and reached out to grab a handful of the straw-like whiskers.

"Ouch!"

Davy giggled at his father's exclamation, and Luke tossed him about playfully for several minutes, finally returning him to the floor.

"Listen. Since Ivan isn't home and I can't go to work in the morning, how about if I take you and Davy shopping."

"I'd love to," Claire responded.

"Good. I got paid a handsome sum for keeling, and we all left Dayton with so little. Make a list of items you and Davy need, and I'll stop by about . . . When can you be ready?"

"Nine o'clock?"

"Good."

With that settled, Luke moved toward the door, and Claire followed. When he turned to say good night, he saw the love in her eyes and felt like a drowning man. Once more the plaguing thought came, *You're go-*

ing to hurt her. "We need to talk. Sometime soon. About the future . . ."

Claire nodded although she did not understand.

As Luke walked back to the docks, he wondered if Claire thought he would be sending her away. Perhaps he should. But that was not what he wanted to do.

Luke, Claire, and Davy walked through the marketplace and toward the shops of Cincinnati. Claire smiled up at Luke under her blue bonnet that matched her eyes, deep as the Mississippi. He had trimmed his beard and looked quite presentable in a crisp shirt that had been laundered and hung in his room awaiting his return. Proudly jostling his son, he returned her smile.

"Sixteen pounds, huh?" Luke asked.

"At least." She grinned up at him.

At times he took her elbow to guide her around holes in the plank walkway or around passersby.

He wondered why he felt so giddy. Was he that much of a landlubber? Was it just the crisp early autumn morning? Or could it be the woman and child accompanying him? This woman evoked a warm feeling from him, as if she touched his very soul. Thinking of his river mates, he smiled. A soulmate. That was a good description for Claire. They had worked together years earlier in the Dayton orphanage, and she had often helped in his ministry. When Miriam died, she was there . . . soulmates. He beamed at her.

Claire stole a glance at him. Her own face reflected the radiance that shone on his.

As their packages began to mount, Luke chuckled. "Perhaps we should have brought a rig."

"Maybe we should call it a day," Claire suggested cheerfully.

"No, not yet. I want to stop at the dressmaker's and buy you a few gowns."

"Oh, no. That's not necessary."

"I insist. Helga Sweeney will probably be glad to get her gowns back."

"I doubt it," Claire answered. Luke looked to her for understanding. "They've all been altered." Then Claire teased, "Surely you don't think we are the same size."

Luke reddened. "No, not at all." His eyes passed slowly over her figure, and Claire was sorry she had spoken so bluntly. "Yours is perfection."

"Luke!" He always had been a tease, before Miriam died.

He laughed. "A compromise then. One pretty gown for the lady who has taken care of my son for three long months in my absence."

Inwardly he rebuked himself, for at his words her expression fell. But there was plenty of time to prove his heart was filled with more than gratitude.

"Very well," she answered.

Inside the shop, a matron hustled to their side to welcome them. "May I help you?" the dark-haired woman asked. She was dressed exquisitely herself, which made Claire blush.

Luke removed his hat. "Please. We are looking for a pretty gown for Miss Larson. Do you think you could help her?"

"Why, indeed! Come right this way, my dear." Claire cast a look of despair over her shoulder, and Luke watched her disappear into a fitting room. The dressmaker then brought several gowns for Luke's inspection. After he selected two, she settled him on a chair with Davy on his lap. She assured him Claire would model the gowns in just a moment.

True to her word, Claire soon reappeared in a blue gown of silk and lace. He watched her finger the skirt with admiration. "That is the one," he said with a wave of his arm. "Don't even try the other one. You look lovely in it, Claire." Then he motioned to the dressmaker. She came closer, and he whispered. With a wink, she hustled Claire back into the dressing room and disappeared. Shortly she returned to Luke with an ivory satin. "How is this?"

"What are you two up to?" Claire called from the fitting room.

"She's finding you something to go with the red scarf," Luke answered.

Claire admonished him. "Luke. You said only one."

"Please, I want to."

Finally leaving the matron and her store behind, they turned a corner where no one was within sight. Unexpectedly for Luke, Claire reached up on tiptoes and set a kiss, light as a feather, upon his cheek.

"Thank you," she murmured.

The innocent act sobered him. "I wish I could do more for you," he mumbled, then wheeled her around and gently took her elbow, directing her swiftly down the walkway. "We'd better call it a day. With Davy, I don't think I could carry another package."

They walked in silence for awhile until Claire asked, "What is it you wished to talk about, Luke?"

He looked at her questioningly, as if she spoke a foreign language.

She continued, "The other night when

you said . . ."

"Oh." Luke slowed his pace.

They were entering a quiet and peaceful residential area. Autumn's first fallen leaves crackled beneath their boots like a campfire and shone just as colorful with tongues of red, orange, and yellow.

"I wanted to talk about us," Luke finally said. Claire's skirt rustled against the parcels she carried, and her cheeks were rosy from the exertion of the long walk. She waited for his explanation. "We need to talk about the future."

"You want to send me away?" she asked.

"No, but I should."

"No? You want me stay and help with Davy?"

Luke glanced sideways at her. Her hair hung long with golden wisps encircling her face beneath her bonnet. She nearly took his breath away. When had he fallen in love with her? Somewhere on the Mississippi, he realized.

Luke set Davy down in a grassy, manicured lawn along with their packages. The child began to play with the brown paper wrappings. Slowly Luke turned to face her. Claire's eyes were so deep, Luke again felt that drowning sensation. "I don't want to hurt you," he blurted out. "If I send you away, which I should, that would hurt you. If I asked you to marry me, that would hurt you, too."

"Marry you?"

"It would be the proper thing to do. After all, we have been traveling companions. But don't you see? We'd be on the run. I could still get hanged. It just isn't fair to ask you."

She reached up and touched his cheek. "You've changed so much. When you went away, you were an empty shell of a man. But you have come back brimming over with life itself."

"I had ample time to think. I guess when one struggles so hard just to stay alive, one begins to appreciate life. Those months keeling, all I could think of was you, Claire. I don't know when it happened."

"Are you saying . . ."

"I love you." They stood just a foot apart, an irresistible force pulling them together. Claire closed her eyes, expecting his kiss, and that was why she did not see the man approach.

"Well, look who's back!"

The despicable voice set the hair on Luke's neck on end. He spun around. "Clancy!" As he faced the repulsive face contorted with glee, Luke's eyes narrowed. "You miserable blackmailer!"

Claire gasped, then rushed to sweep Davy into her arms.

Clancy scoffed, "I ain't gonna hurt the boy. It's his pa I'm after." Then in a malicious tone he taunted Luke. "Thought you could get away, did you? Well, I believe you owe me somethin', and I mean to have it."

CHAPTER 14

Claire descended the Sweeneys' staircase, her chin set in defiance, while Luke paced at the bottom of the landing. For the past hour while Claire put Davy down for a nap, he had gone over every available option. Now his mind was set. When he heard her footsteps, he looked up.

"I've decided. You must go home," he said abruptly. "There's no life for us together. This man means to hound me wherever I go." Luke seethed with anger.

Claire touched his arm. "We could go to the East Coast. Surely the cities are so populated that he'll never find us there."

"You don't understand, Claire." He shook his head. "I've involved you in this too long already."

She ignored his admonitions. "We could change our names." Luke sighed and looked long and hard into her face. It was inviting. Could anyone find them in Boston?

As if reading his mind, Claire suggested, "Or we could go to England."

Luke grinned. Then he pulled her into his arms. "You would be willing to flee the country with me?"

"Oh, yes. I would go anywhere that you could make a new start. I've waited so long for you, I'm not about to give you up now."

"And I've just found you. Perhaps that is what we should do. Go somewhere far away, where no one will follow." He stroked the back of her hair and murmured, "I love you, Claire." He kissed her then, and though his passion ran deep, he was gentle with her for she was an innocent. So sweet and pure.

Ivan, who had been Luke's sounding board for the last hour, peered across his desk. Luke's astounding keeling stories had kept him riveted. Now he listened in disbelief as the younger man detailed his recent encounter with Clancy.

Ivan shook his head. "I just cannot believe that the minute you get back, you are discovered. After all this time. That Clancy is a bad one."

"I agree, but I have a plan."

"Oh?"

Luke felt as excited as a schoolboy. "Claire and I would like to be married as soon as possible."

"You don't say! I think that is a great idea, Luke. Congratulations! So Claire gets in on your next escapade?" At Luke's frown, Ivan quickly added, "I didn't mean any harm in that. Guess maybe I'm just a little jealous of your adventures."

Luke shook his head. "Well, this time I plan to flee the country."

"And go where?"

"I don't know yet. I thought perhaps you could give me some advice."

"Hmm. I may have to think on that awhile."

"We haven't much time. If Clancy turns me in —"

"Yes. I see your position. Did you ever consider missionary work?"

"Why, yes, of course. But what are you thinking?"

"China, India . . ."

Luke leaned back in his chair and rubbed his head. He had not considered anything as drastic as that. "I don't know. I would have to talk with Claire."

"I have contacts. If you could get to Boston, spend the winter there, next spring I could get you on board a merchant ship sailing to the Far East. From there you would be on your own."

Luke moved to the edge of his chair. "Perhaps it's not such a bad idea. It would mean breaking ties with all family, but under the circumstances . . ."

"If you are serious about marrying Claire, I suggest you do it tomorrow. The sooner you are off, the better."

Luke smiled. "I am serious. She said she's loved me all her life. I think perhaps I have loved her for as long as well. I was just too blind to see it."

Ivan was someone he could fully trust. He turned to him now with a question that had been plaguing him for many weeks. "Ivan, is it wrong for me to love again after losing my wife? Sometimes I feel so guilty."

"No, Luke. I believe God has brought the two of you together."

Luke nodded.

The following day a wedding ceremony took place at the Sweeneys' with just a small circle of Luke's friends. The Diagos from the textile mill attended. Maria had deepened her friendship with Claire over the months of Luke's absence, learning the truth of their relationship. Snake-eye stood up for the groom, grinning. Ivan Sweeney waited at the bottom of the staircase to accompany Claire down the aisle.

As she descended, wearing the ivory satin

with the scarlet silk scarf fashioned into a rosebud at her waist, Maria Diago cried tears of joy. Helga held Davy, who babbled, to Luke's delight, "Da-da." The Swedish woman dabbed at her eyes with her handkerchief.

Ivan escorted Claire to the far end of the sitting room, which was arrayed with bouquets of multicolored chrysanthemums, and presented her to the groom. Luke placed her tiny hand in the crook of his arm and gazed lovingly into her Mississippi eyes. Despite all hardships they had encountered, regardless of the dangers they still faced, he thought he would never be happier — his heart never fuller — than at that moment. He believed God in His mercy had lavished upon him more than ample portions of love and blessings.

The ceremony was short, and Luke soon found himself repeating his vow. "I do," he said with emotion.

"Claire Larson," the parson asked, "do you take this man to be your lawfully wedded husband, to honor, love, and obey all the years of your life until death do you part?"

"I do," Claire said, her face a vision of joy.

But just as the preacher announced, "I now pronounce you man and wife," unexpectedly, the front door exploded. A badged man with a drawn gun shouted, "Everybody freeze!" Pointing his weapon at Luke, he turned toward Claire with regret. "I'm sorry, Ma'am, but that part about death may come sooner than you expected. I'm here to take your husband back to hang."

Claire's legs gave way, the room darkened, and she fainted dead away. As Luke moved to catch her, Snake-eye made a dive toward the lawman, who released a shot into the room above Snake-eye's head then pointed it at the keeler's chest. "I said, don't anybody move!"

Maria screamed uncontrollably, and Davy began to cry. Deputy Galloway, backed by a posse of three, barked orders. First to the Spaniard, he said, "You can go, and take that woman with you." He nodded toward the screaming Maria. Then to Helga, "You can leave, too."

"This is my house!"

The deputy frowned. "Can you quiet that baby then?"

Cradling his unconscious, limp wife, Luke glared at the deputy. He nodded at Tony. "Better take Maria and go, Tony. There's nothing you can do."

"Sí, señor. I'm sorry."

With the Diagos gone, the four apprehenders closed the door and gave instructions. "Get something to bring Mrs. Wheeler around," the lawman told Helga. "We'll be taking him to the Cincinnati jail."

Mrs. Sweeney gasped. "Oh, no." Ivan slowly moved to his wife's side.

"Sit down, Dear. I'll get a wet rag." In moments he returned, and Luke dabbed Claire's face with the cloth until she regained consciousness.

"I'm so sorry, Darling," he murmured over and over.

Luke's wedding night was spent under the constant, watchful eyes of Deputy Galloway in the Cincinnati jail.

"You're beautiful," Luke whispered through the bars to his new wife.

"There must be something we can do."

He squeezed her hand. "I'm through running, Claire. It's up to God now."

Her chin rose defiantly. "We must not give up."

"You must go and get some sleep, my love. The days ahead may be demanding."

"But I must keep praying," she protested.

"God knows our hearts. He is able. Let it go, Claire. Go home to the Sweeneys. It is my first husbandly order."

Claire smiled weakly at his attempt at a

joke, and he kissed her good night before sending her off.

Ivan and Helga came to visit the next morning at daybreak, and plans were made to leave Davy in their care so Claire could accompany Luke to Dayton. Ivan offered to send a telegram to Luke's family. The Wheelers thanked the Sweeneys repeatedly for all they had done and expressed regret for the trouble and sorrow they had caused. The deputy then dismissed the Sweeneys with a word of warning about harboring fugitives.

Claire wore her camel-colored riding skirt and white blouse that had been previously packed for their honeymoon. After breakfast, a posse of four set off with their prisoner. Luke's scarred hands were bound, and two armed men rode ahead, one holding Queenie's reins. Luke and Claire, at their dust, were mercifully allowed to ride abreast. The deputy and fourth man brought up the rear.

"I'm sorry they've tied you. It must be painful." Claire spoke softly to her husband of less than twenty-four hours.

"At least I have the joy of you here by my side."

Claire longed to comfort him, to caress that troubled face that portrayed such a brave front. She would be strong, at least until this ordeal was through. "I love you," she said with a valiant smile.

He winked at her. "Hold your head high, Mrs. Wheeler. Don't let them rob you of your spirit or your joy."

"Never!" she exclaimed.

But as the day wore on, Claire and Luke both wilted in their saddles. The posse drove them hard with little consideration given to Claire being a woman. Deputy Galloway would have preferred she stayed behind.

That evening Claire was allowed some moments of privacy. When she returned, she spread out their bedrolls, placing them side by side close to the fire as Luke watched with his bound hands. The night was cold for October, and Claire shivered as they lay their bundled bodies close together.

Deputy Galloway cleared his throat, then apologized. "Sorry, Wheeler, gotta bind your feet at night." Claire's eyes narrowed in the dark as the man tied her husband. "And you," he said, pointing at her, "don't be getting any ideas about setting your husband free, or you'll get tied, too. Understand?"

Claire nodded. When the man left, Luke whispered, "It's all right, Claire. Don't cry now. Be strong. He can't take away our love for each other, can he?"

"No," she sobbed.

"He can't take away our love for the Lord, either. In fact, he is no match whatsoever for Christ Jesus. Whatever happens from now on, remember it must be in the Lord's will for our lives."

"We are in this predicament," she whispered vehemently, "not because it is God's will for us but because of someone else's sin." Claire referred to Ruth Gates.

"Nevertheless, God is in control."

Claire continued to shiver uncontrollably. Luke lay as close as he could and prayed for her, that she would not have to suffer any more than necessary. Davy was young; he would survive. But somehow he must convince Claire to go on without him after . . .

One man stood guard, sitting on a hickory stump, his rifle propped across his legs. His gaze traversed from the fire to the sleeping prisoners, to the deputy and his comrades, to the woods behind them, the road beyond, and back to the fire. But he was no match for the craftiness of the deer-footed keelers who even now crept up behind him.

Snake-eye gave the signal, and his men sprang into action. The one-eyed leader conked the night guard over the head, knocking him senseless. Three others descended upon the camp in a howling invasion. Sure that Indians were attacking, Claire and Luke bolted upright, and the lawmen leapt to their feet. Before they could raise their weapons, the keelers were upon them — some flashing knives, others pointing pistols at their heads.

Snake-eye warned, "Put down your weapons, and nobody gets hurt." Slowly, Deputy Galloway threw down his gun. It was the maniac pirate from the wedding who probably still carried a grudge! The others of the posse followed suit.

"Tie 'em up!" Snake-eye ordered, then he rushed to Luke and cut loose his bindings. "Howdy, Whale." He grinned. "And Mrs. Whale." Claire threw back her head and laughed out loud. With his free hands, Luke pulled her close, tugging her blanket up tighter around her shivering body. "Let's get out of here," Snake-eye hollered.

"I can't," Luke answered.

"What?" Snake-eye and Claire cried out in unison.

Luke turned to Claire then back to Snake-eye. "I won't run anymore. I can't live that way. I've made up my mind to face whatever is in Dayton."

"But, Luke!" Claire shrieked.

"I have to, Darling. If I don't do this

thing, my faith means nothing anymore. I can't explain it. I just know it's right."

"Well, I'll be," Snake-eye exclaimed.

Luke grinned at him. "You were magnificent, like always. But now you need to get your men out of here. I'll give you time to get away, then cut them loose."

"Well, I never. You're sure about this?"

"Positive."

Snake-eye embraced Luke. "God bless you then, Brother."

"And you, my friend."

Snake-eye tipped his hat at Claire, whose face was stained with tears. "Trust him, Mrs. Whale. He's a good man." She nodded, and Luke protectively placed his arm around her. Before Snake-eye left, he gifted Claire with two wool blankets from his own pack.

"It's all right, Claire," Luke said when they had gone. "I know it's the right thing. Come here." They moved closer to the fire and wrapped themselves in the extra blankets where Luke could keep an eye on the tied, gagged lawmen. He gave his mates plenty of time to disappear by ignoring the squirming, mumbling deputy. A tiny Bible provided assurance. By the firelight, Luke read to Claire from the Psalms. When her eyes grew heavy, Luke helped his wife into her bedroll, covering her with the extra blankets.

A few hours before daylight, Luke cut loose the ropes that bound the lawmen. Deputy Galloway jumped to his feet and sputtered angrily, "You could at least have taken the gag off!"

"And listen to you beg me to untie you? The last few hours were most peaceful. Anyway, how could you deny a condemned man a few hours' prayer with his Maker and time alone with his bride?"

"Why did you do it? You could have escaped."

"I'm an innocent man. But I'll not run anymore. God is big enough to see me through this."

"What about her?" the lawman asked, nodding his head at the sleeping woman.

"He is able."

"I see." Deputy Galloway considered his prisoner. Sometime during the night, the deputy's opinion of him had changed. "I don't suppose we'll need to tie you up anymore until we see the skirts of Dayton." He motioned toward Claire. "Better get some rest yourself." Before he turned away, he added, "Wheeler, sorry your wife was cold. You're not the kind of people I thought you were. Guess I was just holding a grudge. Sheriff Watson sure was mad when you escaped under my watch. But I'll see to it that you're both treated with more consideration."

CHAPTER 15

Two days later, just before sundown, the appearance of the six dusty travelers caused quite a stir in Dayton. Folks stopped to ogle. Children ran alongside shouting vicious taunts at the prisoners. One small boy picked up a stone and hurled it at Luke, hitting him in the neck.

"Hey now, stop that. Go on home," Deputy Galloway shouted. But the boys still trailed. Tears streaked Claire's dirty face. Her husband was innocent. Why must he go through such humiliation?

Word spread like wildfire throughout the town. By the time they rode up to the jailhouse, a small group of Luke's friends and parishioners had gathered, including Mary and Gustaf Anders. Luke's face lit when he saw them. The men removed their hats and stretched forth their hands.

Deputy Galloway smiled and nodded at Luke, then cut his hands free. Wearily the

Wheelers moved through the crowd, shaking hands with their friends, embracing and receiving blessings. Claire fell against Mary Anders's stout bosom, and the older woman murmured, "Oh, you poor dear, you poor dear. They going to let you come home?"

"I don't know, Mary."

Sheriff Rusty Watson watched from the threshold of his open doorway. His brows furrowed in disapproval when Deputy Galloway cut Luke's bindings. He hoped that this reception would not get out of hand. "Let 'em pass through now!" he called loudly. No one seemed to hear, but after several tense minutes he closed the door behind his prisoners. Sliding the bar across it securely, he breathed easier.

"Pleasure to see you again, Reverend," he greeted as he led them to the barren cell that Luke had previously occupied. With the Wheelers behind bars and the key twisted and removed from the lock, Sheriff Watson leaned against the wall.

"There's no reason to lock up Claire!" Luke said in exasperation.

"I need a few minutes with my deputy," Sheriff Watson replied. "Then I'll be back."

Luke left Claire standing alone in the middle of the cell and went to the barred window to look out. In a few minutes he would know his fate. Was there any hope?

Sheriff Watson turned to his deputy. "What's the story, Galloway?"

"If I'd have believed the man was innocent, I might not have worked so hard to capture him. I guess I was set on revenge because he made a fool of me the night of the jailbreak."

"You think he's innocent?" the sheriff asked, surprised.

"I do. Wait 'til you hear what happened."

Upon hearing Deputy Galloway's full explanation, starting with his prisoner's wedding day and including Luke's honorable behavior when the keelers tried to break him free, Sheriff Watson returned to Luke's cell.

"You're free to go, Mrs. Wheeler." Relief washed across Luke's face. "You can stay with the Anderses. There'll be a private hearing where you'll be required to answer some questions. But I'm afraid short of a miracle, your husband will hang day after tomorrow at noon."

"No!" Claire screamed. "He can't! He's innocent!"

"That may well be, Ma'am, but the law is final."

Luke drew Claire into his arms, and she

wept on his shoulder. The sheriff said with compassion, "I'll give you a few minutes alone, then Mrs. Wheeler will have to leave. Let me know, Reverend, when she's ready." He left them alone.

"Claire," Luke murmured against her hair, "I need you to be brave."

"No! We can't let this happen. Our life together is just beginning," she sobbed.

"Perhaps the Lord did not intend for us to be together this way. If I hadn't escaped the first time, you wouldn't have been pulled into all of this. I wouldn't have brought such shame upon you."

"Don't talk this way, Luke," she begged, pulling on his arm. "I won't let them take me away."

Luke's eyes narrowed, and his voice came out much louder and sterner than he had intended. "You must!"

His command sobered her. "I–I'm sorry," she whimpered, struggling to gain her composure.

"That's much better." Luke lifted her face, and she looked at him through blurry eyes. "Perhaps you can contact Simon Appleby for me."

She nodded. "I–I'll do that right away."

"Thank you." He gave her a quick embrace, then released her as he moved toward the barred door.

"Sheriff!"

Sheriff Watson appeared, then led Claire out of the jailhouse. As she departed, the sheriff called after her. "Of course you know you're not to leave Dayton."

"Of course," she replied calmly. As she looked around, she saw no one she recognized. She headed toward Simon Appleby's office. It was a good distance, but she needed the time to think.

"Simon!" Luke exclaimed. "You're a welcome sight."

The two men embraced, then Simon spoke right at the heart of the matter. "I think I have good news. I got your telegram about Clancy. He's the one who tipped the law on your whereabouts. When I got your telegram, I'd hoped you wouldn't return to Cincinnati."

"I was there only a few days. In fact, I would have been gone by the next day. I had to see Claire and Davy."

"That's what they expected you to do."

"What's the good news?"

"At my insistence, Clancy has been apprehended. He's being brought to Dayton and should arrive tomorrow." Luke's eyes lit with understanding. "As soon as he arrives, I'll ride out to the Gates place. His testimony, the fact that we'll have proof Aaron Gates murdered Silas Farthington, may persuade them to tell the truth."

Simon stroked his mustache. "With Ruben as an accomplice to that murder, he may not want to add your death to the list of offenses he'll be tried for. Since our time is limited, if Clancy doesn't arrive by noon tomorrow, I'll go ahead and do what I can to force a confession."

Meanwhile, Luke's father and brother, Ben, rode into Dayton. Before they approached the crossing of Main and Third Streets, Emmett heard the familiar, horrible sound of scraping boards and pounding nails.

"Come on!" He urged his horse forward. Just as he thought, three men were working to reconstruct the gallows for Luke's hanging. Ben's usually ruddy face paled. "Father?"

"Let's hurry."

Only minutes later as Simon was leaving the jailhouse, they jumped from their mounts and hastily tied them to the hitching post. Emmett ran toward the familiar attorney. "Simon? Is that for Luke?"

"I'm afraid so," Simon answered. "I've just been with him. I'm going to do my best to get him freed. Luke can tell you. I must go now."

"I understand. God go with you." At the barrister's departure, Emmett and Ben hurried inside. When they were ushered into the inner room where Luke's cell was, they found him standing with his back to them, stooping to gaze out the barred window.

"Luke?"

He whirled at the familiar and beloved voice. "Father! Ben!"

Sheriff Watson did not smile when he told the elder man, "Hope you don't mind if I don't trust you inside the cell this time, Reverend." Although it hadn't been proven, he knew that Emmett Wheeler had helped his son escape.

Emmett smiled sheepishly while the sheriff pulled up chairs for Luke's family. Hands gripped hands through the bars. Tears trickled down all three faces, but Luke quickly brushed his aside. He was astonished at his own strength; however, he knew the Lord was giving him an ample portion of faith for this hour to face death.

"Father, Ben, did you know that Claire is now my wife?"

"Yes, we heard. That is wonderful news, Son."

"Because of me her life is ruined."

"You only returned her love, and love surpasses all. Be assured, Son, we'll take care of her and Davy."

"Thank you. How is everyone?"

Ben answered, "Heartsick with what's been happening to you, Brother. But otherwise well."

Later that evening, Emma Cook climbed out of bed to see where Uriah had gone. When she heard the familiar voice of their neighbor, Ruben Gates, she ducked behind her bedroom door, eavesdropping.

Her husband boasted loudly, "You ain't got nothing to worry about, Ruben. They'll hang him high this time. Then it'll be finished." She shuddered at the look of vengeance upon his face.

"He'll get his just deserves."

"I hope you're right."

The door slammed then, and the voices grew fainter. Emma Cook took a deep breath. She thought back to the day when Aaron Gates had been killed, when she had stayed with Ruth and the conversation she had overheard. She began to tremble. Sitting back on the edge of her bed, she rocked herself, murmuring unintelligible phrases.

The door slammed again, and she slipped beneath her covers, feigning sleep as her whistling husband entered the room and pulled off his boots.

Puffy-eyed, Emma Cook prepared breakfast for her cheerful husband. The eggs sizzled in the skillet, and the coffee brewed on the top of the stove. Uriah stepped close behind his wife and grabbed her by the waist. "Morning!"

"Good morning, Uriah. You're happy today."

"Yep. Got good cause, too."

Provoked at knowing what that good cause was, she smacked the eggs rather hard onto his plate, and the yolk of one broke, but her voice remained calm. "What's that, Uriah?"

"The law brought back the runaway preacher. He's to hang tomorrow noon." He then looked at the plate set before him. "You broke my egg."

"Sorry, Uriah."

Silence lingered except for Uriah's scraping fork, and after Emma had poured coffee into brown mugs, she seated herself across from him.

"It's not like you to be on the wrong side of justice. You've always been a fair, honest man. A good man." Uriah glared up at his wife as she said, "But you're wrong in this.

You know that preacher is innocent."

He slammed down his fork. "You're just like my mother, falling under the preacher's spell." He stood up and pointed a thick finger at her. "You stay away from that devil! You hear? I lost my appetite!" He pushed back his chair and walked to the door. Before he went out, he turned back to his wife and said in a much lower tone, "I thought better of you, Emma. Truly I did."

Claire lingered over her morning tea with Mary Anders. The older woman wanted to know everything about their trip. She was an extremely emotional listener, but Claire trusted the woman's good counsel.

"I wonder how Davy's doing," Claire murmured.

"I'm sure he's fine." Mary stirred the sugar into her second cup of tea as she stole a glance at Claire's distant stare. Curiosity provoked Mary to change the subject. "I sure was surprised to hear that you and Luke got married." She motioned with a dimpled hand. "I'm glad you could find a bit of happiness in the midst of all this."

"Oh, Mary," Claire confided, "it's not like that. I think Luke just married me because it was the proper thing to do. We'd spent so much time together alone. When I ended up going with him, he was worried about what people would think."

Mary showed surprise at Claire's confession. "But, Dear, I know a look of love when I see it. And I saw it in Luke's eyes. He's not the same man who left here. Why, he adores you."

"There was a time I thought perhaps . . ." Claire turned her face away from Mary.

"Yes?"

She sighed. The woman would not let it lie. "He told me several months ago that he would never love again, that he was an empty shell of a man. But when he returned from keeling, I thought he'd changed. He even told me he loved me."

Mary Anders looked puzzled, and Claire tried to explain, "But looking back, now I understand. He knew I'd get hurt no matter what, so he did what he thought was best by me. I think he married me to protect my reputation."

Mary tried to reason with Claire. "Of course you have doubts when you didn't even get a honeymoon. All new brides do. If you'd been allowed any time alone with him, you'd know he loves you."

Claire shook her head with its neatly coiled braid. "No! He had the chance to escape. We could have left the country and had a life together. But he chose to hang. Don't you see? He chose death . . . over me." Her voice broke with emotion, but she blurted out the rest, "He still wants to be with Miriam. He knew all along I'd be released from this marriage by his death."

Mary rose and moved to Claire, patting her back. "Now, now. You can't go on thinking such things, Claire. I believe your imagination is working overtime. I know for a fact that Luke is a very honorable man. If he told you he loved you, then he does."

"He always treated me like a sister," Claire cried.

"Because he's a proper gentleman."

"No. He's been cool toward me."

"He's under a lot of stress right now. I'm sure he's just trying to prepare you for the worst."

Claire stood to face Mary. "If I lose Davy, too, I don't know what I'll do."

"Lose the child? Why would you?"

"Ben is here. Luke always talked about Davy going to live with him. Ben and Kate, my cousin, can't have children of their own. They have already adopted two boys. I imagine they think Davy would complete their family just fine. But they can't have him! He's mine now!"

Mary gripped Claire's shoulders. "Claire,

stop this! I know the stress is awful for you, too. But you're just talking nonsense! Now get yourself ready, and go visit your husband. You tell him your doubts. For your own peace of mind, you must get this settled."

Claire shook her head. "No. He already has so much on his mind, how can I cause him more grief? Oh, Mary, I'm so confused." Claire moved into Mary's arms and accepted the comfort they afforded.

The loose, dry earth billowed upward from the pounding horse hoofs, covering Emma Cook with a cloud of gagging dust. Nevertheless, she continued at a fast clip, often looking over her shoulder to see if Uriah pursued, until she entered the outskirts of Dayton. She straightened herself in the saddle and guided her mount through the traffic until she came directly in front of the building marked BARRISTER SIMON APPLEBY.

Carefully she tethered her mount and approached. Her heart pounded, and her husband's angry voice echoed in her mind. *You're just like my mother, falling under the preacher's spell. You stay away from that devil! You hear?*

Nevertheless she proceeded. Before entering she brushed off her clothes and straightened her bonnet. The door was unlocked and swung open freely, groaning eerily. The room inside was dark and empty, except for a mammoth desk, masculine furniture, and rows of books.

With a sigh, she whirled to leave and nearly collided with Simon Appleby, who stood in the open doorway. She gasped.

"Mrs. Cook, I'm sorry if I frightened you. May I be of help?"

The woman's voice trembled. "Are you still the preacher's attorney?"

Simon's heart leapt. "Yes, I am." He took a few steps into his office, closed the door behind them, and drew open the window coverings. "Come. Sit down and we'll talk."

"Thank you." The thin woman took the seat offered and waited, her face expressing pain.

"Now. What can I do for you?" he asked kindly.

"The preacher didn't kill Aaron Gates."

Simon slid to the edge of his seat. "Why do you say that?"

"If I tell you, can you help me?"

"Yes. You have my word."

"My husband will be furious when he finds out I came. He's really a very good man. But this whole thing — it's like he's not himself. I–I don't know what to expect from him."

"I understand. Sheriff Watson and his wife often provide housing for witnesses. I'm sure you'd be welcome to stay with them for awhile, if it comes to that. Or I can go with you to talk to Uriah."

Emma wrung her hands. "Thank you."

Simon smiled encouragement. "What do you know?"

"That day when Uriah hauled the preacher in to the sheriff?" Simon nodded. "Well, he stopped by home and told me to stay with Ruth. When I got there, I overheard her and Ruben talking. You see, Ruben and Aaron had been arguing. When Ruth tried to intervene, Aaron hit her. Ruben tried to help her and pushed Aaron hard. He accidentally killed his father. Then when the preacher came, Ruben went out the window."

Emma looked down at her hands. "I should have told the truth at the beginning, but I didn't want to go against my husband. When I told Uriah, he told me to keep quiet. Then when the reverend escaped, I thought it would be all right."

"Why did Uriah testify against Rev. Wheeler?"

Emma's face saddened. "When he was a

small boy, a preacher ran away with his ma. All the time he was growing up, he heard his pa talk about slick-talking preachers. He was good friends with Aaron. Aaron didn't want Ruth going to church. Before his death, he'd been filling Uriah's head with nonsense about Rev. Wheeler."

Simon nodded. "I understand."

"He warned me this morning not to side with the preacher. He won't understand. He's just not himself right now."

"Don't worry, he'll come around."

"But that isn't all. Ruben came to the house last night. I don't know what they're up to."

Simon reached across his desk and took Emma's hand. "You are a very brave woman. You have saved an innocent man's life." Emma hung her head shamefully as he spoke to her. "If I go with you, do you think you could tell your story to the sheriff?"

Emma's face took on a new look of determination. "I've come this far. There's no turning back now."

"Good. Someday there will be another trial, and you will be called on to testify. I will stand by you all the way and see personally to your safety."

"I understand."

Simon released her hand then and rose, going to her side. "Mrs. Cook?"

She also rose and followed him out. He turned toward her again with a reassuring smile. "It's just a short walk."

CHAPTER 16

Sheriff Watson knocked on the door and waited, exchanging glances with Simon, who removed his hat.

The door swung open, and Ruth Gates placed her hands on her hips. "What do you want?" Her rude question left a scowl upon her face.

"May we come in?" Sheriff Watson asked.

"I'll come out. I don't like to upset the children, although Mr. Appleby seems to delight in it." Her sharp look stabbed Simon, but he did not offer a rebuttal.

Sheriff Watson asked, "Is Ruben here?" Ruth reddened slightly and nodded toward the barn. "Out there."

"I'd like for him to be in on our conversation. Shall we walk that way?"

Ruth shrugged her shoulders and led them toward the barn, calling out to warn her son when they were within hearing, "Ruben, Sheriff Watson's here!"

She stopped several yards from the barn, and Ruben appeared in the open doorway, rifle in hand. He leaned against the wooden frame. "You here to tell me that you're finally going to hang my father's murderer?"

"I don't think you'd like it very much if we did that, Ruben."

Ruben straightened. "You're wrong. It's exactly what I want. Justice."

"But then it would have to be you standing on the gallows tomorrow."

Ruth's eyes darted from her son to the two intruders. Simon was watching her, ready if she made a move; however, she stood rigid and motionless.

"That's very funny," Ruben sneered.

"No, it's not. We have evidence that you struck the blow that inevitably killed your father."

"That's not true!" Ruth denied. "It was the preacher!"

"Evidence, pooh!" Ruben spat on the ground at his side.

"Emma and Uriah Cook know the truth," Sheriff Watson said.

"No!" Ruth screamed.

Sheriff Watson turned to answer her, and Ruben used the opportunity to hoist up his rifle and point it at the sheriff while he edged away from the barn, moving toward his horse.

"You'll not get far," Simon shouted.

"We'll see."

Before he could mount, Ruben heard the cock of several guns behind him and whirled toward the sounds. Deputy Galloway and two others stood, ready to shoot. "Drop it, Ruben."

Simon grabbed Ruth by the arms, restraining her, while Sheriff Watson confronted Ruben. "Why don't you tell us the truth for once? I'm not itchin' to hang anyone. You can trust us, Ruben. We want to help you."

Ruben didn't reply. Sheriff Watson continued, "We've got Clancy's story and Emma Cook's. Now let's hear your side of the story."

Ruben closed his eyes and nodded.

Ruth began to sob.

That evening a group gathered at the Anderses' home. Mary had cooked a celebration supper as soon as she heard of Luke's release. Now they conversed in the sitting room, going over the day's astonishing events.

"Aaron Gates was not a bad man," Simon explained. "He began to have terrible headaches and eventually took to the bottle to relieve the pain. Ruth said that was when his character changed. He couldn't handle his liquor."

Luke turned to his wife. "I found out the whole story about Clancy." Claire tilted her head, listening attentively. "One night on board the *Hilde,* Aaron was in a stupor and beat up an employee, Silas Farthington. He threw his unconscious body overboard. Ruben was there at the time and tried to save the man, but he never surfaced — he drowned."

"And Clancy saw it?" Claire asked.

Luke nodded. "Yes. He began to blackmail Aaron."

Simon interrupted. "But first Ruben left Dayton. He was tired of watching his dad go downhill."

Luke continued, "Clancy found Ruben in Cincinnati and tried to blackmail him as well."

"But that didn't work," Simon interjected. "Ruben returned to talk the situation over with his father."

Gustaf Anders rubbed his balding head. "That was what they were arguing about the day you visited the Gateses, Luke?"

"Yes," Luke agreed.

"Mercy me. Such a sad thing," Mary murmured in her usual way.

Simon further explained, "Ruth Gates

tried to intervene, and Aaron struck her. That frightened Ruben, and he pushed his father away. There was a bit of a struggle. Aaron fell, hitting his head on the edge of a chair. I don't believe any of it was intentional."

"I just happened to arrive at that time." Luke gestured with a wave of his hand. "And Ruth sent Ruben out the window. Later when Uriah appeared, Ruth conveniently put the blame on me."

"Why would Uriah lie about the hanky like he did in the courtroom?" Emmett asked.

"Because he hates preachers." His bearded chin in his hand, Luke pondered his own statement.

Simon explained, "Uriah's mother ran away with a preacher when he was a small boy. His own father drilled it into him that preachers were liars, womanizers, and bad. At first he simply believed the worst of Luke. Later he just wanted revenge for that one in his past."

"Oh, how sad," Claire said. "I'm so glad Emma had the courage to come forth with the truth." She looked across the room at the attorney she had grown to respect. "Do you think Uriah will forgive her?"

Simon nodded. "Yes, I think he'll come

around. But the trial could be a painful one."

"For all of us," Luke said. Slowly he continued, "And then there is the pain of forgiving."

Claire added, "The Lord's portions are ample. He has seen us through so much already. Surely He will help us forgive."

After Simon had gone home, Luke said to the others, "I'm really tired. I think I'll go out to my place tonight. It's been empty for months. I just need some time alone to sort through things."

Claire felt a lump constricting her throat. Everything had happened so fast. She had not thought about their life together. Had she expected him to stay with her tonight? She felt Mary's gaze upon her and blushed.

Luke walked to her then, gently removing her hands from her lap. Caressing them, he said, "It's been a long day for all of us. Get some rest tonight. I'll be by in the morning, and we'll make plans." He kissed her lightly on the cheek. Claire remained sitting, her back stiff.

Gustaf saw him to the door. "I'm so pleased this is over. God bless you, Reverend."

When he had gone, Claire gave Mary an I-told-you-so look and fled up the stairs to her room.

CHAPTER 17

Luke lit a candle in the dark house and looked around at the familiar rooms, furnishings that he and Miriam had picked out. He moved into the kitchen and fingered once again her apron hanging on the peg. He'd never had the heart to pack away her things. Now he wished he had.

Slowly he made his way through the cobwebs into the bedroom. He took a deep breath. There on the bed lay a dusty black valise, packed and ready for the trip he and Davy never took. Davy's cradle was missing. He remembered. Claire had taken it to the Anderses' home.

Claire. He knew he could not bring her to this house for their first night together, not with Miriam's things still here. Anyway, the place was filthy, like he knew it would be. He had seen the hurt in her eyes, but he was just too weary to deal with it tonight.

She knew he loved her, and that was all

that mattered. Tomorrow they would make plans to go on a honeymoon. He would ask Mary to pack up Miriam's things. It would be better that way.

He set the valise on the floor, undressed, and climbed into bed. Weary as he was, he thanked the Lord for bringing him through this terrible time. He prayed for Davy and thanked God for Claire. Then he drifted off, dreaming of his new wife.

The following afternoon was hot for late October. The sun shone brightly through the lofty but nearly bare oak and elms, providing a blanket of warmth over the sparkling autumn meadow. Luke and Claire lounged on a woolen striped blanket, strewn with multicolored leaves and picnic remains.

"Come here, Darling, closer," Luke coaxed.

Cautiously Claire moved closer, their shoulders touching. Luke stretched his arms out toward the sky. "It feels so good to be a free man."

"You're not exactly free," she corrected.

His brows furrowed. "Why not? Are you thinking of the trial? Sheriff Watson said I could come and go as I pleased as long as I was here for the trial."

"I imagine that will be a few weeks away." Claire sighed.

"Does it trouble you?"

"No. That wasn't what I meant. You're not exactly free because of our marriage," she murmured so softly he strained to hear.

He cupped her chin in his hand. "But that's the best part."

Claire burst out, "Luke, I wish you would not pretend so. I know why you married me." She gulped. "I know you don't love me."

"What?" Luke was so astonished he dropped his hand and stared at her, unable to find his tongue.

She rattled on. "I'll never be a burden to you. I'll not ask you to love me. And I'll do my best to be a good mother to Davy."

"Why I know you will, Darling." As he looked at her jutting chin, so determined, and her quivering pale cheeks, he suddenly understood.

He took her hands in his again. "Listen, Claire, to what I tell you. I loved Miriam and grieved at her loss. You know I did. What I said that night about never loving again . . . I guess I was just plain blind."

Two tears trickled down Claire's velvety pink cheeks. He longed to reach out and brush them away, but could not bring himself to release her tight grip upon his hands.

"I guess God in his wondrous mercy had other plans. He unlocked my heart again and allowed me to love you. I dreamed of you every night when I was keeling. I missed you terribly. I discovered I was in love with you all along. Now I know I even loved you as a little girl with pigtails. I love you as I've never loved anyone before. Can you believe me?"

"I–I don't know. It's so sudden."

"Sudden? After all these months to-gether?"

"The realization of it is."

Luke pulled her close. He kissed his wife with all the fervor he felt. She gasped and stroked his cheek. With delight she said, "Why, I believe it's true! You do!"

He laughed, throwing back his head. Then he captured her hand, "What about you, Claire? Do you feel burdened to be shackled to me?"

"Why no. I'm happy, I'm . . ."

He waited for her to say the words. The truth of those words several months ago had given life to his own dormant feelings. She could not refuse his pleading eyes.

"I love you, Luke. I always have."

"I'm a fortunate man. Can you forgive the

many times I spoke to you so heartlessly, threatening to send you home?"

"You tried to do what was best."

He looked out across the meadow. The slight breeze occasionally sent brittle leaves swirling downward to the earth.

"Luke?"

"Hm?"

"Can you forgive the Gateses, the Cooks?"

Luke smiled. "I already have." Claire looked surprised. "Last night when I lay in bed, I counted my blessings. Well, of course, God brought that to mind. I struggled with it for awhile. But I so want for you and me to have a perfect start. I couldn't let anything hinder our chances. Do you understand?"

"Yes."

Luke recalled as did Claire some of those times they shared over the past few months. In doing so, he remembered his disguises. With a sudden cheerfulness, he turned to her. "So tell me, Mrs. Wheeler, what do you think of my new look?" He turned his face from side to side, a broad grin enveloping his face.

Claire touched his smooth chin. "I like it. Now I can see all your dimples."

He gave her a thank-you kiss, then coaxed, "Why don't you lay your head in my lap while we discuss our honeymoon plans."

Claire blushed but acquiesced. "What do you have in mind?"

"Do you think you'd mind terribly if we camped out, like we did so many times together?"

She sat upright. "I'd love it. The weather has warmed."

"It could turn cold again."

"We'll have each other to keep warm," she ventured.

"We could honeymoon our way to Cincinnati, visit our friends there, pick up Davy, maybe stop in Beaver Creek and visit family."

"Oh, yes." She nodded with enthusiasm. "I'd really like that."

"Then we could come back and settle in here," he suggested. "There would be the trial, of course."

"You know your congregation will want you back. What will you do?"

"I'll talk it over with my beautiful new wife, and together we shall decide."

Claire snuggled her head back onto his lap. "She'll probably say she wants you to return to your pastorate."

"I thought she might." He looked down at her, his heart aflame with ample portions of love and desire.

ABOUT THE AUTHOR

Dianne Christner and her husband make their home in Scottsdale, Arizona, enjoying the beauty of the desert. However, it is fond memories of her childhood spent in Ohio that inspired this book. After years of working as an executive secretary, she is happy to be able to spend her time at home writing or traveling and researching. If you enjoyed this book, she invites you to visit her Web site www.diannechristner.com so that you can meet her and her family members and follow her latest writing endeavors.